Justin Strikes

The Unknown Inflictor

Justin Strikes: Book One: The Unknown Inflector

A.C Ham © 2021

Bogart, Georgia

abbyhamauthor@gmail.com

Cover design by Abby Ham

I feel like there are so many people I owe thanks to, but there will be more books for everyone to get their share, so this one only has two.

First of all, to the "supercarlinbrothers" A.K.A, J and Ben. I have no idea if you will ever see this but the intro for one of your videos inspired me to create a new world for people to dive into, so truly, none of this would have happened without y'all.

And second and most importantly, to Mrs. Paula and Mrs. Kristy. The two of you are some of the best teachers I've ever had and this book wouldn't have gotten here without your advice and encouragement.

Contents

Chapter One
A Strange Occurrence

Justin stepped on his shoelace, fell, and lay sprawled across the school hallway. What a great start to his Wednesday.

"Watch it!" a girl scoffed, stepping over him.

"Sorry," Justin mumbled, trying to move out of the way, which is hard to do when people are walking by and over you from both directions.

"Here," a boy offered his hand to help him up.

"Thanks," Justin accepted his hand and stood.

"No problem," the boy shrugged as he walked away.

"Just shake it off," Justin thought, squaring his shoulders as he continued making his way down the hall. *"It could have been way worse."*

And then it got worse: someone called his name.

"Yo! Lil Tyke!" called Bobby.

Bobby "the Bruiser" Johnson was notorious for his teasing and because he was the smallest of the eleven and twelve-year-olds, Justin was the main victim of Bobby's jokes.

"Where ya going?" Bobby asked, cracking his knuckles.

"English," Justin sighed.

"Don't talk back to me!" Bobby growled.

"You asked a question," Justin mumbled.

"What'd you say, Pipsqueak?"

"Nothing," Justin fought the urge to roll his eyes.

"That's what I thought," harrumphed Bobby. "See you later, Mouse."

"Always a pleasure Bobby," Justin mumbled as Bobby headed off in the opposite direction.

"Hey, Justin!" Someone called from behind him. "Wait up!"

Justin turned to find his friend Sam pushing through the sea of kids.

Sam, like Justin, was small. However, unlike Justin, Sam had a constant manic look in his eyes that had helped him make a reputation for himself as the class hooligan. His frequent gags included stealing whiteboard markers, drawing on his face with a pen, or trying to tape things in his dirty blond hair.

"'Scuze me, coming through," Sam said. "Outta my way."

He squirmed past a girl, accidentally knocking her over.

2

"Oops! Sorry, Mary!" he gave her a sheepish look before turning to Justin. "I've got bad news."

"What?" Justin asked, anxiously biting his lip.

"Mr. Plumes' car got keyed, so he's in an especially bad mood today."

"Great," Justin sighed. "Just what I need, a teacher who hates me in a bad mood."

"Yeah… Tough luck," Sam shrugged.

Lunch

"Dude," Sam said, sitting down with his tray. "Mr. Plumes is on a warpath."

"It's true," interjected Tammy. "In fourth period, he sent three kids to detention for no reason!"

"Really?" Justin asked, shifting uncomfortably in his seat.

"Yeah!" Sam nodded. "I heard that one of them was chewing gum and he threatened to send them home! For chewing gum!"

"That seems harsh," Justin frowned.

"I told you!" Sam said, slamming his hands down on the table. "*Warpath!*"

Math class

The clock ticked by, seemingly slower and slower as if the day would never end. Justin started to believe that he'd be stuck in math forever. The clock's slowing tick-tock echoed in the room, its hands taunting Justin with their ever-slowing movements.

Out of the twenty-two students, Justin felt the least noticeable. Other than Bobby and Sam, no one paid attention to him. Well, his friend Franklin used to, but he'd enrolled in a different middle school, so Justin didn't see him as often. Being small made Justin particularly easy to miss and his mousy brown hair didn't help him stand out in the slightest. The only remotely interesting thing about him was his emerald green eyes, which had caught the attention of his kindergarten teacher who had said, "Oh what beautiful eyes!" and his second-grade substitute who told him "You remind me of a character in a book I've read, he had your eye color." People used to stare into his eyes for a second longer than he was comfortable with, but then Justin got good at avoiding eye contact.

Despite being overlooked by his peers, his teachers took special notice of him. "Ah, Justin Strikes. Terrence's little brother. Terrence was a wonderful student, I expect a lot from you!" They were usually disappointed. Not to say Justin was a bad student, he just wasn't the prodigy Terrence seemed to be.

Like a majority of the kids in Wednesday's eighth-period math class, Justin was not paying attention to Mr. Plumes's lesson. However, unlike his peers, Justin was entertaining himself by twirling his pencil in between his fingers. In between twirls, he tapped the pencil on the desk.

Whirl whirl. **Tap.** *whirl whirl.* **Tap.**

"So if 'X'," Mr. Plumes wrote on the board. "Equals twelve-" **Tap.**

"and 'Y' equals-" **Tap.** Mr. Plumes glanced Justin's way.

"Seven. What does-" **Tap.** He looked annoyed, but Justin didn't stop.

"'Q' equal?" **Tap.**

"Mr. Strikes!" His face grew red as he raised his voice. He took a deep breath before continuing. "Unless you are taking notes, I suggest you put that pencil down."

There were sniggers from behind him.

Justin dropped his pencil on the desk with a sarcastic flourish.

"Thank you," Mr. Plumes nodded at him before turning back to the whiteboard. "Now, who knows the answer?"

Justin immediately grew bored. As one tends to do when bored, Justin let his mind begin to wander. He could see it now, Daydream Justin would aim, wait until he was positive that he'd hit his mark, then hurl his pencil at Mr. Plumes.

"Not in a lets-hope-he-gets-stabbed-in-the-eyeball kind of way," Justin thought to himself. *"But just enough to make him look stupid. Like a hit in the middle of his forehead that everyone happens to see."*

There was a tingling sensation in his fingers, followed by a noise like *"whooom"* and the pencil disappeared from his desktop.

"What the heck?" Justin whispered, leaning forward to look for it on the floor.

Whoom. There was a blue flash of soft light over his shoulder. The pencil was there, floating in midair.

Before Justin could comprehend what was happening, the pencil was soaring through the air, heading straight for Mr. Plumes.

Time seemed to slow even further as the pencil tumbled through the air, gaining speed before- **BAM!** It hit Mr. Plumes in the middle of his forehead as he turned to address the class.

Mr. Plumes slammed his hands down on the desk.

"Alright!" he yelled, slamming his hands down on his desk. "Who threw that?"

Silence, followed by someone coughing.

"No one?" Mr. Plumes faked a gasp. "Well, as far as I know, it's impossible for something to throw itself. So one of you better come clean or else I will have you all suspended."

Justin took a shaky breath.

"Well... It was nice knowing you world," he thought to himself as he raised his hand.

"It was me."

Mr. Plumes let out a long sigh and rubbed his forehead.

"Mr. Strikes," the teacher groaned. "Well, I can't say I'm surprised, but I am disappointed."

"Gee, never heard that one before," Justin said inwardly, resisting the urge to roll his eyes.

Mr. Plumes grabbed a pad of paper and started writing as he walked towards Justin's desk.

"Take this," he ripped off the page "to the principal's office."

Justin felt his heart drop to the soles of his feet.

"Yes sir."

Chapter Two
False Crimes and Fair Punishment

The waiting area outside Mr. Herring's office was cold and reeked with the rancid scent of Ms. Hartfield's flowery perfume.

Justin fidgeted in his seat, which emitted a loud squeak.

Ms. Hartfield looked up from her typing.

"Mr. Herring will be done soon," she said in a honeyed tone that matched the honey color of her cardigan. "He's wrapping up a call with a parent."

Justin nodded as she went back to her typing.

"Was it a lapse in memory?" he wondered. *"No. It couldn't have been. It just… Disappeared. Then it was floating!* It was like witchcraft!"

"What's that hon?" Ms. Hartfield asked.

"Great. I said that out loud," Justin could feel a blotchy blush spreading across his cheeks.

"Nothing," he shook his head as the door to Mr. Herring's office opened.

"Justin?" Mr. Herring said, popping his head out of the door. "You can come in."

"Okay," Justin muttered. "I can do this."

"Don't worry," Ms. Hartfield smiled as Justin stood. "He doesn't bite."

Justin gave her a half-smile and followed Mr. Herring into the office.

Mr. Herring's office

"Justin Strikes, eleven years old," Mr. Herring read from a file on his desk. "You've been attending J.B.W. Middle for a year..." he looked up from the folder. "Can you tell me why you're in my office today?"

"Well, sir," Justin looked down at his hands. "I-um... I threw a pencil at my teacher."

"I see," he leaned back in his chair and gave a knowing nod. "And why did you do that?"

"Um... Teenage rebellion?" Justin winced at his stupidity.

"MmHm..." Mr. Herring squinted at him, his beady eyes barely visible. "Are you sure there isn't any other reason?"

"No sir," Justin mumbled.

He took a deep breath, deciding to go the sob story route. "But Terrence left for boarding school and I'm left with a couple of nine-year-olds... It's just kinda..."

9

"Hard to get used to," he thought.

"Like you're the man of the house," Mr. Herring guessed.

"...yeah," Justin mumbled.

Mr. Herring sat back in his leather-bound chair, his beetle-like eyes studying Justin's face.

"Well," he started. "I think it's obvious that this was just a one-time occurrence. I will call your guardians and letting them know about the incident. I'll leave it up to them to decide on your punishment, however, I think it would be appropriate if you wrote Mr. Plumes an apology. Does that sound fair?"

"Yes, sir."

120 Two Bridges Street, after school

Justin stood on the Willows' front porch, dreading the punishment he was about to face.

"Are you going in, or are you going to stand there like a high school kid waiting for his prom date to answer the door?"

Justin turned to face his godsister.

"You know, for a nine-year-old, you have a lot of sass," he rolled his eyes.

10

"I know." Rose placed her hands on her hips. "I read a lot of books with sassy characters, so I picked up a lot of one-liners. Besides, they don't just move you up a grade for being smart... Though it helps."

"She's right you know," said William, Rose's twin, joining them on the porch. "Besides, it's not like they're going to kill you… Well on second thought..."

"Oh shut up, Will," Rose shoved him. "They're not going to kill him."

Justin sighed, taking in the sight of them. Rose and Will were both fairly tall for their age, with their dark hair messy from soccer practice. Other than the sprinkling of freckles Will's nose, Rose's raspberry-colored glasses, the differences in their hair length, and the fact that Rose was far dirtier, they were similar in every aspect, from their hazel eyes to their matching soccer jerseys.

"Well?" Rose asked, impatiently. "Can we go in?"

"Yeah, let's go," Justin said, releasing another shaky breath.

"Woohoo!" cried Will, turning the doorknob and racing into the house. "Let's watch Justin face certain doom!"

"Shut up, you're not helping Will," Rose scolded as she followed him into the house.

Mrs. Willows was waiting for them in the kitchen.

"Hey, kiddos!" She smiled as they dropped their backpacks on the table. "How was school?"

"Pretty good," Rose unzipped her bag and began looking through it. "Mrs. Rosenfield taught us what idioms are and the class couldn't make heads or tails of it!"

"Very funny," Mrs. Willows laughed. "Will, how about you?"

"It was okay," he shrugged. "Larry Cumbers let me eat some of his chips at lunch and then Jenny fell into a trash can and I almost died laughing. And then, of course, Justin got in trouble."

"William," Mrs. Willows frowned. "We don't laugh at other people's misfortunes."

"Sorry," Will tried to look remorseful, but Justin could tell that he wasn't. "But even Jenny was laughing as she tripped! She had a milk carton on her head!"

"That doesn't give you permission to laugh," Mrs. Willows shook her head, trying to get the image of Jenny with a milk carton on her head out of her mind. "How about you two go get changed while I talk to Justin."

"Oooh! Someone's in trouble!" William sang.

"William," Mrs. Willows sighed. "Go."

Will laughed and ran upstairs, humming a song about a guy in jail as he went. Rose followed after whispering a quick "good luck" to Justin.

"So," Mrs. Willows said, crossing her arms. "Your principal called."

Justin looked down at the tiled floor.

"Do you want to talk about it?" she asked as he refused to meet her eyes.

"Not really," Justin whispered.

Mrs. Willows squatted down and scanned his face.

"We'll talk about your punishment when Mr. Willows gets home," she sighed.

Justin nodded, his hands anxiously gripping the straps of his backpack.

Mrs. Willows' face softened.

"Go get started on homework," she said gently. "I'll call you down when he gets here."

"Okay," Justin whispered, his eyes wet for no reason.

Mrs. Willows leaned forward and pulled him into her lap. Justin sobbed into her shirt as she held him, feeling a mixture of confusion, overwhelmedness, and anxiety.

"We're not mad," Mrs. Willows said. "I promise, we're not. We just want to know what's going on."

"I don't know what's going on," Justin said inwardly.

Mrs. Willows pulled away. "We're just worried."

Justin nodded.

"I know," he sniffled.

Mrs. Willows nodded and squeezed his shoulders.

"I love you, but go blow your nose and get started on homework."

Justin nodded again and trudged upstairs.

Chapter Three
The Hidden Society

"Justin, why did you throw a pencil at your teacher?" Mr. Willows asked.

Do you know what's fun about a stressful day? When it doesn't end (that's sarcasm by the way).

After being sent to the principal's office for a crime he wasn't sure he committed, dealing with his peers either judging or congratulating him on said crime, and having to do math homework… Let's just say Justin started crying again.

"I- I don't know…." Justin choked on the lump in his throat. "I don't know what happened. It was- It- It was like…"

"Breathe," Mrs. Willows took a deep breath, moving her hands, motioning for Justin to do the same.

Justin breathed in... And out. Slowly the lump in his throat receded.

"It was like… magic," he said, feeling dumb for even thinking the words.

"Magic?" Mr. Willows repeated, adjusting his glasses.

"Yeah, I mean…" Justin stopped. "I was thinking about throwing the pencil, but not seriously considering it. And then next thing I knew, it had hit him in the head."

"Do you think it was one of the other kids?" Mrs. Willows asked.

"No, it was *my* pencil," Justin lowered his voice. "It was on my desk and then… it just disappeared. I don't remember throwing it."

"What do you mean it *disappeared*?" Mrs. Willows asked. "Disappeared how?"

"I don't know," Justin looked down, his eyebrows knitting themselves together as he tried to recall the strange event. "It was on my desk, then- then there was a sound, like a puff of air… And I looked down and it wasn't on my desk anymore."

His eyes started to water again at how fake the next part sounded.

"Then there was a flash of blue light and it was hovering above me..." he took another deep breath. "Then it went flying… And it hit Mr. Plumes in the face..."

Justin felt a tear fall down his cheek.

"Am I crazy?" he whispered.

Mr. and Mrs. Willows looked at each other, silently having a conversation before turning back to their godson.

"Let's talk in the office."

The Willows' home office

Mr. Willows locked the door behind them.

"You might wanna sit down," Mrs. Willows said, motioning to one of the desk chairs.

"Am I in trouble?" Justin asked, trying to ignore how badly he was shaking as he sat.

"Yes… and no," Mr. Willows turned to Mrs. Willows.

"You're in trouble," Mrs. Willows said. "But we don't think it was your fault."

"You know that nine years ago…" she said, sitting on the floor. "There was an attack downtown."

"The one my parents were in," Justin said, his voice raw.

Mrs. Willows nodded.

"Right," her voice was tinged with sorrow. "It's what messed up their minds and made them… unwell. But there's a reason they were attacked."

Justin froze, hardly daring to breathe out of fear that he'd wake up from this dream.

"The official statement said the attack was targeted at a visiting dignitary, but that was just a coverup. The real reason was that your parents were working on something. Something that someone didn't want anyone to know about and was willing to kill to cover up their efforts."

"Why?" Justin frowned, all of this was new to him. Up until this moment, he'd thought his parents were casualties from someone else's revenge.

"Your parents were a part of a secret community," Mrs. Willows paused, frowning slightly. "Do you remember those comics you and your brother used to read? The ones about superheroes."

"Yeah… Why?" Justin's frown deepened.

"The community... It's kind of like that," she shrugged.

"A secret community… Of superheroes…" Justin looked from her to Mr. Willows, then back again. "Is this a prank?"

Mr. Willows laughed. "This went so much better when we told Terrence."

"It's not a prank," Mrs. Willows assured.

"So what does this have to do with me?"

"Well…" Mrs. Willows made a face and shrugged. "Your parents were…"

"Superheroes?" Justin gaped.

"Their term for it is Ablete," Mrs. Willows corrected.

"Ab-Leet?" Justin tested the unfamiliar word.

"It's Latin, I think," Mrs. Willows added.

"My parents were Abletes..." Justin stared at her. "What does that have to do with my pencil?"

"It means that you might... have powers."

That night: after dinner

Justin knocked on the door to his mother's room.

"Hello?" she called from inside. "Someone has arrived to help me hunt!"

"Mom?" Justin said, undoing the locks on the door. "I... It's me. Justin. I have your food."

"Justin!" She shouted gleefully.

He opened the door to find his mom standing on her bed, holding a glass of water with buttons in it up to the ceiling.

"Mom! What are you doing?" he set down the food and rushed forward to grab her arm.

"Well the bats in the attic said I was a traitor for talking to the squirrels outside, so I'm trying to lure them out so we can have peace talks." she stepped off the chair.

Justin sighed. His mom had good and bad days. This was a bad day.

Clarissa Strikes, who usually lived at a "wellness center" was staying at the Willows household after something at the center had caused her PTSD to flare up. The staff at the wellness center was trying to take steps towards preventing another incident but thought it would be best if she stayed off-campus until they were done setting up new preventive measures.

Clarissa Strikes didn't look much like her youngest son. Her hair was a lighter shade of brown, her eyes were hazel, like Terrence's, and she was tall instead of short. Yet Justin had his mother's cowlick..

"Mom…" Justin said, shaking his head to set aside the comparison and sitting in front of the door. "Can you tell me about the Abletes?"

Her eyes glazed over as she stared at the wall.

"Mama?" Justin asked, wondering if she had heard him.

"Once," she began, "when I was thirteen, my parents took me to a carnival. There was a Ferris wheel, a juggler, and a pretzel cart! After we left, I was so hopped up on sugar, because I ate three cinnamon pretzels, that my mom made me run sixty-five laps."

"Sixty-five?" Justin said incredulously.

"I *loved* running!" she started tapping her finger on the bedpost. "I was so fast, the fastest in my class. My favorite teacher once told me that on top of being one of the smartest students, I was one of the fastest."

"Mom…" Justin said, putting together the pieces. "You had superspeed?"

"Yes! It was the most special of my abilities." she tapped her finger faster, glaring at the ceiling. "If only those pesky bats thought so."

Justin looked around the room.

The sealant around the window, the worn-out carpet, the dulled edges of the bedpost. The room was fixed so she couldn't hurt herself and had once been as familiar to Justin as his own, but now he was noticing new things about the room.

There was a small worn place where she was tapping her finger, the curtains were in bad shape as if they'd spent years being whipped around the wind, and the carpet was worn out in patterns as if it had been walked in the same pattern continuously.

"Mom?" she stopped her finger tapping as he spoke. "Can you still run that fast?"

She gave him a mischievous smile. Then, *Woosh!* The room filled with a tornado-like wind as she became a blur.

Justin turned his gaze to the floor and, sure enough, she was running the same pattern on the rug.

That night: living room

"So... what now?" Justin asked his godparents as soon as Rose shut her bedroom door upstairs.

"What do you mean 'what now?'" Mr. Willows asked.

"What now?" Justin repeated. "What happens now that I have powers?"

"We," Mrs. Willows started. "You finish out the school year, then next year you'll attend C.A.P.E.S."

"Capes?"

"Yeah. It's an Ablete school. I think it's near the town your grandfather lives in."

"There's more than one Ablete school?"

"There's six I think..." Mrs. Willows frowned.

"Is Capes where Terrence is?" Justin asked, interrupting her wondering.

"Yes," Mrs. Willows smiled. "All of the Ablete children are required to go to an Ablete school once their powers develop, so as soon as we knew Terrence's had come in we enrolled him at Capes."

"Where is Capes then?" Justin asked.

"Georgia," Mrs. Willows explained. "Though I don't know exactly where."

"Why not?" Justin frowned.

"I'm not an Ablete, that information isn't for me," Mrs. Willows shrugged.

"Then how come you know some of this stuff?" Justin asked.

"When I was in high school, your mom saved my life," Mrs. Willows explained. "But in doing so she revealed her powers to me. Normally, people without powers aren't allowed to know anything about the Abletes, so your mom broke some rules in revealing herself to me. After the incident, one of her Ablete friends gave me some information on what you and Terrence would need in order to join the other Abletes."

"Justin," Mr. Willows said, his tone serious. "The twins can't know about the Abletes."

"He's right," Mrs. Willows agreed. "As I said, your mom broke some laws by telling me."

"Okay, but…" Justin tried to choose only *one* question to ask. "But what if something like what happened today, happens again?"

"It won't," Mrs. Willows firmly said. "You'll be careful to not do something like this again. Besides, it's only a month till school ends and then after summer, you'll go to Capes."

Chapter Four
Preparations and Clues

There were no more incidents… well sort of.

"I still can't believe Mom and Dad are still letting you go to boarding school after you put a dent in the wall," Will said.

"It's harder to force-lift an apple than you'd think," Justin thought.

"Maybe they're sending him as a punishment," Rose quipped.

Will smiled. "I wonder what Terrence did to make them send him away..."

"I wonder what you'll have to do to make me the only child in the house," Rose giggled.

"Hey!" Will interjected.

"Justin!" Mrs. Willows called from downstairs. "You almost ready?"

"Yeah," Justin stood. "I'm ready."

Somewhere on a road in Tennessee

Justin gazed out the car window, his eyes tracing the lines of the trees they passed.

"How much longer?" he asked.

"Three minutes," Mrs. Willows said.

She glanced his way.

"Justin, I know you wanted to visit, but..." she sighed. "Just don't expect him to hold a conversation."

"I won't get my hopes up," Justin promised. "I just want to see him before I leave."

St. Allen's Home for Mental Wellness

"Hi! How can I help you?" asked the man behind the counter.

"We're here to visit Gerald Strikes," Mrs. Willows pulled a slip of paper out of her pocket. "Room number... 320."

"Okay..." the man (whose name tag read 'Henry') typed something on his keyboard. "May I ask how you know the patient? This patient can be visited by family."

"This is his son, Justin," Mrs. Willows motioned towards him. "And I'm his guardian."

"Can I see some I.D?" Henry asked.

"Of course!" she pulled her driver's license and Justin's school I.D. out of her bag and handed them to

Henry, who compared the information to what was on the computer.

"Everything seems to check out," he handed them their I.D.s. "You're good to go."

Room 320

Justin entered the room to find one of the nurses reading his dad a book.

"Hi!" she smiled. "Mrs. Willows and... Terrence, right?"

"Hi, Cindy!" Mrs. Willows smiled. "This is Justin."

"Right," Cindy nodded. "Terrence is the one who brought the stuffed lion. Justin brought the family portrait."

She pointed to a drawing taped to the wall.

Justin smiled at the scribbles. "I remember that."

Cindy turned to Mrs. Willows. "I'll let you two have some privacy."

She left.

Gerald Strikes always looked tired when Justin visited. His dark hair was messy, his t-shirt was slightly rumpled, and his green eyes were unfocused and bleary, with dark lines under them. At the moment he was sitting in his chair by the window, staring somewhere between the window and the woods outside.

"I'll give you two a minute," Mrs. Willows said, easing the door shut behind her.

Justin forced himself to walk further into the room and sit on the floor in front of his father.

"Hey, Dad. It's me... Justin."

Gerald continued to stare out the window.

"I'm leaving for Capes next week. I'll be where Terrence is."

His dad mumbled something.

"Mama's doing well... As well as she can anyway. There was another incident, but she seems to be doing relatively well otherwise."

"Clariminasosheef," Gerald mumbled.

"I think Terrence is doing well," Justin continued. "He doesn't call much and he didn't come home for summer break, so I don't really know..."

"Juh."

"Yeah..." Justin nodded listlessly. "The Willowses are doing good. The twin's team won their tournament, Mr. Willows got a raise, and Mrs. Willows is hosting the book club this month."

No reply.

28

"I guess I'm a bit nervous about leaving. I'll be away from home for…" he drew a deep breath. "For a while. It's just… I don't know. It's a lot."

Tears threatened to pour from his eyes, but he blinked them away.

"So… yeah," he gave his dad a half-hearted smile.

He went on to explain what he'd been doing all summer (which was a lot of playing video games, tagging along to the twins' soccer games, and trying to get more information about his new school). He took his time to over-explain as much as he wanted. He was in the middle of telling him about his efforts to try and brush his teeth with his powers when a knocking rang from the other side of the door.

"Justin?" Mrs. Willows called from the hall. "We need to leave soon, we have errands to run."

"Okay," Justin called back. "I'll be out in a minute."

He turned back to face his dad. "I guess I've got to go. I'll be back for Thanksgiving and Christmas, so I'll see you then… I love you Dad."

He stood and went to open the door.

"Love… You… Too."

Justin turned, his eyes brimming with tears.

"Thanks, Dad," he sniffed, ignoring his tears as he wrapped his arm around his dad.

He was about to let go when his dad's grip turned to iron and his eyes cleared as he fixed Justin with a stare, a sense of urgency brewing behind his pupils.

"Red... Box... Backfake... Secrets... 65... 20. 2... 9."

Justin pulled back.

"What?" he gasped.

His father turned away, facing the window as his eyes glazed over again.

Justin turned away, wiping the remainder of his tears and confusion away before opening the door.

"Hey, how'd it go?" Mrs. Willows asked as he stepped into the hallway.

"Good," Justin shrugged. "He spoke a bit."

"Oh!" Mrs. Willows nodded."What did he say?"

"Gibberish mostly... But he also told me he loved me."

Mrs. Willows smiled sadly.

"Good," she said, forcing a happier smile. "That's wonderful, sweetheart."

Her smile turned sad again as they headed for the elevator

"I remember when Terrence came by last year," she said, pressing the down button. "He had been going through something... I think he was hoping Gerald would say something to him. When he came out he said that Gerald had said a total of three words. Whatever the words were, Terrence deemed them important."

Justin looked down at the elevator floor.

"Must have been pretty important for him to not bother visiting this summer."

"Justin," Mrs. Willows chastised, shaking her head. "You should be happy for him. A fifteen-year-old with straight A's? I'd say dedication is a good reason to skip *one* summer with the family. Plus, he's acing driver's ed, made friends who were willing to invite him over for the summer, *and* he calls every week."

Justin sighed. "I guess...I just wished he'd take a week to visit."

"Me too," Mrs. Willows nodded. "Me too."

Chapter Five
Details and Departure

To: Justin Strikes

From: Capsburg Direction Academy

The following is the recommended packing list, along with a list of prohibited substances.

Packing list:

- ❏ Backpack

- ❏ Pre-order books (Booklist on page three)

- ❏ Pencils (Standard number two) and other standard school supplies

- ❏ Other essentials (i.e clothes, toiletries, etc.)

Please note that toys, books, and other personal items are also allowed, but must be sent to main offices, not brought with students.

"How stupid is this list?" Will laughed as Justin pocketed the book list. "Don't bring cigarettes and drugs. Like, duh!"

Rose rolled her eyes at her brother, taking the list from his hands to give it back to Justin.

"I'm pretty sure I have all of this already," Justin said, passing the list to Mrs. Willows.

Mr. Willows nodded. "We'll make sure you're stocked up on essentials before you leave and most of your textbooks have come in. we'll make sure you have money for… your other class books."

"The classes for my powers," Justin supplemented silently.

"Other than that, you should be good to go," Mr. Willows finished.

"You're sure you're not missing anything?" Mrs. Willows asked.

"Nothing that comes to mind," Justin shrugged.

"Okay!" she smiled. "We'll finish packing up your room today and send ahead the stuff you'll need."

Justin nodded.

"I can't believe you're leaving," Rose said. "I mean, 'yay! One less person using our bathroom,' but… I'm going to miss you."

Justin laughed.

"I call dibs on his room!" William smiled.

"No!" Rose groaned.

"William. Rose," Mr. Willows warned. "You already have your own rooms, neither of you is getting Justin's room."

William frowned.

"I still think you should've sent Justin into the army," he joked. "But either way, it's going to be lame without you here."

"Really?" Justin asked, genuinely surprised.

"Yeah." William nodded seriously. "Who else is going to bring me snacks during soccer?"

"I do that," Mrs. Willows frowned.

"Who's going to help me with my math homework?" Rose asked.

"Me," Mr. Willows said.

Rose scrunched up her nose.

"You're bad at math," she complained.

Justin smiled.

"Well at least I know I'll be missed," he said.

"If you're going to get all sappy, I'm leaving," Will grimaced.

That night

"Have you called Terrence?" Mrs. Willows asked.

"No..." Justin said as he sat down in the living room.

"Okay." She grabbed a box from the side table. "Well, you're going to be able to now."

She placed the box on his lap. Justin blinked at the picture of a phone on the lid.

"It's already programmed with my, Mr. Willows, and Terrence's numbers," she said as Justin opened the box. He blinked in surprise when he found an actual phone inside.

"It's mine?" he said, glancing up at his godparents.

"Yes," she smiled. "Now, it's not the latest model, so it doesn't have all the features, but it's yours."

"Thank you," Justin said, grabbing the phone from the box.

"You're welcome," she smiled. "Now go call your brother."

35

Upstairs

"Hello?" a voice said through the phone's speaker.

"Hey, Terrence," Justin said, forcing himself to stop pacing the room to sit on the edge of his bed. "It's Justin."

"Justin!" there was a shout in the background. "Hey, little brother what's up?"

"Not much…"

"Start with the important things," he thought to himself.

"I'm going to Capes next week."

"Yeah, I heard," Terrence said, unsurprised.

"Yeah- I- um…" Justin grasped for something to say. "I discovered my powers by accidentally throwing a pencil at my teacher. It hit him smack dab in the middle of his forehead."

"On… accident?" Terrence asked.

"Yeah… I was just thinking about it and then the pencil disappeared and then it was floating."

"Might be telekinesis…" Terrence mused. "Which teacher was it?"

36

"Mr. Plumes, he was *so* mad!" Justin laughed. "It hit him square in the face. I had six people congratulate me on my aim. He was mad at me the rest of the semester, which is stupid because I got all the questions he asked me right…"

There was silence on the other end.

"Anyways… I visited Dad today," Justin continued.

"Oh…" Terrence paused. "How is he?"

"Spacey," Justin admitted. "But he spoke to me."

There were yells from Terrence's end of the call.

"Terrence?"

"What did he say?" Terrence said, his voice a whisper behind his friend's shouts.

"He mumbled some gibberish and told me he loved me."

"Ah." More silence.

"It wasn't much…" Justin admitted. "But it was nice to hear some sort of a sentence."

"Mmhmm…" Terrence said, his voice tinged with anticipation. "Listen, Justin, I've got to go. Matt and I have plans."

"Oh. Okay…"

"I'll talk to you later," Terrence said.

"Bye," Justin said to the dial tone.

Midnight

"Ugh, this is too hard," Justin groaned, flopping backward onto his bed and throwing an arm over his eyes.

"You need to concentrate," Justin whispered to himself. *"You've got this."*

Justin sat up, refocusing on a pack of gum on his desk. He closed his eyes and imagined the pack floating towards him.

"Focus," He muttered.

There was a sound of tires on pavement.

Justin paused, trying to regain his focus.

Something on the left side of the house creaked.

He waited for the pack to land on his outstretched palm.

Nothing happened.

"I give up," Justin groaned, getting up to use the bathroom.

Justin stumbled through the dark hallway and made his way to the bathroom.

He closed the door and fumbled for the switch.

"There it is," he mumbled as the room filled with light.

Justin scanned the shelves for a headache pill, found the bottle, filled a paper cup with water, and took one.

He went to turn off the light.

"What?"

The light switch was off.

Justin looked up at the light fixture.

Instead of a hazy yellow, the light shone a pale, blue.

Justin turned back to the switch and flipped it on.

No change.

He tried to turn it off.

Nothing.

"I wonder..." he muttered.

Justin moved the stool underneath the light and stepped up. Carefully he stretched his hand towards the light.

The light flickered out, leaving him alone in the dark.

"Weird," he shrugged, making his way back to his room.

Chapter Six
Arrival and Eliza

"Okay, we have your suitcase in the car," Mrs. Willows said, counting on her fingers. "Your boxes were sent ahead, I have your registration papers, do you have your duffle bag?"

"Yep!" Justin pointed to where it sat on the couch in the living room.

"Okay…" Mrs. Willows clapped her hands together. "Well, then we can hit the road."

Justin nodded, grabbing his bag from the living room and slinging it over his shoulder.

He gave a hug to Mr. Willows and turned to the twins, who were strapping on their shin guards.

"Good luck at tryouts," he said, hugging Rose.

"I don't need luck." Will smirked. "I have skill."

"He needs prayer, not luck," Rose joked as Justin gave Will one last noogie.

"I'll miss you guys," Justin laughed, shouldering his bag.

"We'll miss you too," "That's lame," the twins replied.

Justin laughed again and followed Mrs. Willows to the car.

Somewhere outside of Memphis

"So," Mrs. Willows said, turning down the radio. "Once we get to Memphis, I'll drop you off at a phone booth that will get you to Capes."

She pulled a slip of paper out of her purse.

"This paper had a code for you to use," she handed it to him. "Then… I don't know, it'll take you to your destination."

"A phone booth," Justin repeated.

"Yes," she glanced at him. "I don't know how it works, but Terrence did it, so… Piece of cake right?"

"Piece of cake," Justin nodded.

A phone booth in Memphis

The phone booth was red, like the kind you would expect to see in London. Maybe it was from London because it looked as if it had made a long trip to get here. Its paint was peeling in some places and the numbers "22231-1211-120" engraved on the side were well-worn.

"You've got the code I gave you?" Mrs. Willows asked as she pulled his suitcase out of the trunk.

"Yeah," he opened his palm to show it to her.

42

"Good," she placed the suitcase inside the booth. "I'll wait here for five minutes to make sure it worked... You ready?"

Justin nodded, unsure but hopeful.

She enveloped him in a hug.

"You'll be fine," she promised before pulling back, tears glimmering in her eyes. "Promise to call, okay?"

"Okay," he smiled. "I love you."

"I love you too, Justin."

Justin stepped into the phone booth and closed the door.

The inside was just as old-looking as the outside was. The windows were covered in a green-tinted layer of grime, the keypad was so worn that the numbers were almost entirely gone, and the floor was littered with trash.

Justin took a deep breath and stared down at the piece of paper in his hand.

210 706 67853: Turn over for directions to C.A.P.E.S.

Justin punched the code into the number pad, wincing at the loud click each button emitted.

After he put in the last number, the phone booth filled with the sound of wind, so loud it sounded like a hurricane was outside. Justin's ears popped as the door was replaced by a swirly purple and blue door.

Then, the phone rang.

Justin closed his mouth, unaware that it had fallen open, and picked up the receiver.

"-tal. To arrive at your destination step, through the portal. To arrive at your-"

Justin hung up the phone, grabbed his bags, and stepped through the portal…

Somewhere else

…And into another phone booth.

This phone booth was newer, almost shiny, and was more crimson than scarlet-colored. There wasn't any trash on the floor, the numbers on the keypad were legible, and the windows were clean with a frosty tint. There was a sticker with a smiley face on the door that read "Capsburg Phonebooth #3 is happy to see you."

Justin released a shaky breath, grabbed his bags, and opened the door.

"Woah," Justin gasped, his jaw-dropping.

Skyscrapers rose all around him, each one tinted a different color of the rainbow. They looked aerodynamic as they reached for the heavens, the shapes they had were something from a science fiction

44

movie, they seemed to flow as they sat stationary. The building behind the phone booth seemed to be twisted as if a giant had tried to wring it out, the one across the street's windows was a glassy peach color that, combined with the building's rounded corners, made the whole complex look like a giant can of peach soda.

What surprised him more than the peculiar buildings were the people he saw. Most of them looked normal, the guy walking by looked just like his neighbor Joe, but a few commuters were dressed in what looked like armor, like a superhero's suit. A woman jogged by talking to someone on her phone, dressed in black leggings and what looked like a silvery kevlar vest. A guy drove by in a minivan that had a sticker for "MR. STUPENDOUS' DAYCARE" on its bumper.

"You know, it's rude to stand in the middle of the sidewalk," said a voice to Justin's left.

Justin turned to see a girl his age standing with her hands on her hips.

"Sorry," he said, blinking in surprise at her appearance.

She had an icy blue streak in her long, dark hair that made Justin notice the flecks of blue in her muddy green eyes. Her outfit was more peculiar. First off, she was wearing jeans, which was perfectly normal, but the dark green jacket she had on had a golden zipper in a zigzag pattern, like a lightning bolt, and made Justin's head spin as he tried to fathom how the zipper was functional.

45

Her mouth twitched into a smirk as he moved to the edge of the sidewalk.

"At least you're nice enough to move," she shrugged, messing with her bag as she joined him on the side of the walkway. "I'm guessing it's your first time in Capsburg."

"Yeah, how'd you know?" he gasped.

"A lot of people stare on their first visit," she gazed at the city around her before looking at him again. "Are you going to Capes?"

"Yeah, are you?" he asked, hope swelling inside his chest.

"Of course!" she raised one of her eyebrows. "Why else would I be here?"

"How should I know?" he joked. "I'm new, remember?"

She smiled, genuinely this time. "Wanna tag along with me to Capes?"

"She's a stranger," a voice in Justin's head warned.

"She's my age," Justin argued.

"Sure!" He adjusted the handle of his suitcase. "I'm Justin."

"Eliza," she smiled again, leading the way down the sidewalk.

"Are you from here?" he asked, hurrying to follow her.

"Nah," she scrunched up her nose playfully. "I'm from a Leet city near North Carolina. My aunt lives here though."

"Leet?" Justin frowned.

She glanced at him before answering.

"It's a slang term for Ablete," she explained. "Norm is slang for Non-Ablete people and Lune is what we call people who got powers in other ways."

"Oh," Justin nodded slowly. "Cool."

They paused at a crosswalk, waiting for the light to change.

"How about you?" Eliza asked, her gaze fixed on the crosswalk sign. "Where are you from?"

"A Norm town in Tennessee."

"I'm not bad at this slang," Justin said inwardly.

"Have you always lived there?" she asked as the light changed.

"Technically," he answered, trying to remember where he had lived before the attack as they crossed the street.

"I think we lived in an apartment," Justin thought, trying to recall. *"Somewhere downtown. At least we did before the attack…"*

"Oh," Eliza said, her voice sad. "I'm sorry, I didn't know. It must be hard not remembering."

"Yeah," Justin grew solemn. "I don't remember how my parents were before… Wait! How did you do that?"

"Oh my gosh! Shoot!" she grimaced, giving him a chagrined look. "I'm sorry. One of my powers is mind reading. I can't control it yet."

"Oh, okay," Justin forced a laugh. "For a second there I thought I had gone crazy."

"Imagine how I feel," Eliza groaned. "Hearing people speak without them saying anything."

There was an awkward pause as they crossed another street.

"So… Do you have any siblings?" Justin asked as they turned a corner.

"Yeah, three sisters," she gave him a half-smile. "My mom says her stubborn Latino side helped her win the lottery in having four daughters. How about you?"

"I have a brother and two Godsiblings."

Eliza frowned. "What's a Godsibling?"

"It's your guardians' kids. My guardians are my Godparents and their kids are my Godsiblings," he realized he was about to ramble and forced himself to take a breath. "If your parents can't take care of you, they adopt you and become your family God gave you, your God family."

"Ah," Eliza watched a guy in a lime green jumpsuit pass by. "Do you get along with them?"

"Most of the time," Justin shrugged. "The twins can be annoying, but we've been closer since my brother left to come to Capes."

"I get that," Eliza nodded. "I've never really been close to my older sister, but I'm pretty protective of Kara and April. They're four and two and… Oh! Here's the road to Capes."

As the buildings got shorter and more small town-like shops took over the block, more and more people flooded the sidewalks. The majority of them were school-age kids heading for a long cobblestone road between two of the shops at the end of the block.

"Wow," Justin said, watching the scattered students walking down the road. "Do parents ever walk with their kids?"

"Not really," she shrugged. "It's kind of a tradition for kids to walk the path themselves. Only the overprotective parents walk with their kids. You know, the kind that is so overprotective they might as well be an umbrella."

Justin giggled, as Eliza smiled and rolled her eyes.

"Come on," she said, walking towards the road. "We wanna get in line before rush hour starts."

Chapter Seven
C.A.P.E.S

"Why is everyone just standing there?" Justin asked as they approached a swarm of people.

Eliza groaned, glaring at the people blocking the road.

"The main gate has a scanner so students can use their I.D. to get in, but because no one has this year's I.D. yet, everyone has to be signed in manually."

Justin sighed. "This is going to take a while, isn't it?"

A while later...

"Please get in the line that corresponds to the *first* letter of your *last* name," called a girl holding a megaphone. "The table on the far left is for last names that start with A through F. To the right of that we have G through M. The next right is N through R. And on the far right we have S through Z."

Eliza headed towards the last line and Justin followed, rushing to dodge other kids getting in line.

Another while later...

"Last name?" asked the guy sitting at the table at the end of the line as the person in front of Eliza made their way past the gates.

"Thistle," said Eliza.

"O-kay," he flipped through the pages on his clipboard. "First name?"

"Eliza."

"Okay," he checked off a box. "You're good to go. Next?"

"Hi," Justin said nervously.

"Hi," the volunteer smiled. "Last name?"

"Strikes."

"Okay..." he flipped through more pages. "First name?"

"Justin," he picked at one of his fingernails as the volunteer crossed something off the page.

"Okay. You're all set. Next?"

Justin passed by the table to where Eliza was waiting for him in front of the gate.

"Ready?" she asked.

"Not really," Justin admitted.

"Admitting you're not ready is the first sign that you might be," Eliza smiled. "Or at least that's what my mom says."

Justin's laugh got caught in his throat as he took in the school.

"Woah..."

Justin and Eliza stood on a cobblestone path, between two large fountains. In front of them, covering a large expanse of the grassy lawn, was a sleek, white building. It had multicolored windows that glittered like fish scales and seemed to be six stories tall, but Justin was pretty sure that he was exaggerating. Two slightly smaller buildings peeked out from both sides of the front building, the similarities they shared to the larger building made them look like her twin children.

Justin scanned the rest of the property. To their left was a small forest of pine trees and in the backmost corner to the right was a series of hedges.

Eliza noticed his gaping and smiled.

"Cool school, right?" she said, nodding approvingly at the campus.

"Yeah," Justin nodded.

"It gets better after the power ceremony," Eliza declared.

"Power ceremony?" Justin asked.

"Yep!" Eliza said, heading down the path. "Come on! We'll be late!"

"Right," Justin shook his head, trying to focus. "Let's go."

Outside of Capes

In the wall over the main entrance was a marble carving of two Abletes in cloaks flying in a circle around each other. The engraving under the carving read:

Capsburg Ablete Power Enforced School

"Oh..." Justin realized. "Capes is an acronym."

"Yeah and a pretty dumb one," Eliza said, entering the building. "I'm pretty sure Ablete means power and *everyone* knows it's a school. Besides, what powers are they even enforcing?"

"Hi, there!" A chipper voice interrupted Eliza's criticisms. "Welcome to Capes!"

A red-headed girl was waving to them, her rosy smile softening the features of her egg-shaped head. She clicked a pen against the clipboard she held as she walked over to them, her bright yellow cardigan flapping in her wake.

"I'm Amber, I'm a fifth-year here," she said. "I'm guessing you two are first-years?"

"Yeah," Justin nodded.

"Awesome!" she smiled. "Well, welcome to Capes! Let's get your bags labeled and put with the others, they'll get put in your rooms during the ceremony along with whatever stuff your parents sent separately."

"Amber," another volunteer said, walking over. "I've got some labels and I'm heading that way, so I can put their bags with the rest so these two can skip the line."

"Okay, awesome!" Amber smiled.

The volunteer, whose name tag read Timothy, handed them labels and pens. Justin and Eliza put their names on the labels and stuck them to their bags.

"I'll take these," Timothy said, taking their luggage from them.

"And you two are free to go to the auditorium!" Amber smiled.

"Where's the auditorium?" Eliza asked.

Amber scanned the crowd behind her.

"Valerie!" she called.

A girl, maybe twenty-five, turned around and frowned at Amber.

She had curly brown hair that bounced as she made her way towards them and purple glasses that reminded Justin of Rose. Unlike Rose, she looked like she was constantly in a bad mood.

"Yes?" she asked, putting on a painfully fake smile.

"Could you take these two to the auditorium for me?" Amber asked, glancing at the students coming through the door. "I've gotta make sure that the other first-years get their luggage checked."

"So am I," Valerie frowned. "Besides, how hard is it to say it's at the end of either hall?" she turned to Justin and Eliza. "Big room. Can't miss it."

She walked away before Amber could come up with a retort.

"Thanks," Eliza said, making her way to one of the halls on the side of the giant staircase in the middle of the foyer.

Justin followed her down the hall and into the auditorium at the end of the hall.

The auditorium was the size of a theatre auditorium and included a carpeted stage and rows of folding chairs.

"Where should we sit?" Justin asked, trying not to gape at the size of the room.

Eliza scanned the room and pointed to one of the rows in the middle.

"How about there?"

56

Three minutes later

"Do you know what happens at orientation?" Justin asked Eliza as the chairs slowly filled.

"Orientating?" she guessed. "I think it's mostly just a ceremony to figure out what the first-year's powers are."

"Oh," Justin nodded, a thousand more questions popping into his head. "So what powers do you have?"

"That I know of... Mind reading and telekinesis."

"What's Telekinesis?" Justin asked.

"Moving things with your mind."

"I have that!" Justin exclaimed.

One of the kids in front of them turned around to give him a weird look.

"I mean..." Justin blushed. "I can do that."

"Yeah, it's a kinda common ability," Eliza shrugged.

"If something like telekinesis is common what would be uncommon?" Justin wondered.

Chapter Eight
The Ceremony of Powers

Half an hour passed, everyone in the auditorium had long ago grown bored. Half of the room was chatting idly, while the other half tried to find something to do on their phones. Justin and Eliza were just beginning to run out of conversation topics when a piercing screech rang from the speakers.

Justin looked up and saw a tall woman in a white dress standing at the microphone that had been set up on stage, laughing awkwardly as the room gave her their attention.

"Well… I guess the mic works," she said, tucking a loose strand of her caramel-colored hair behind her ear.

"Welcome everyone to the Capsburg Ablete Power Enforced School or, as we call it, Capes," she smiled. "We're about to get started with our ceremony but first, a few words from our principal, Mr. Erik Whitaker."

She stepped away from the mic, leading the room in a round of applause as a middle-aged, balding man climbed the stage.

"Thank you, Miss Andromeda," he said, fixing the audience with a fixed smile that made Justin squirm in his seat. "And hello to all our first-year students! As is a custom at our school, I have prepared a speech."

There was a mass groan from the crowd, but Mr. Whitaker ignored them.

"Our motto, 'utiliser le pouvoir bien' has been the building blocks for this school since the beginning. For those of you who can't understand all languages, it means 'use power well'. I like to think that…"

Mr. Whitaker continued his speel about campus rules and whatnot, but no one was listening. As soon as the lecture started, Eliza pulled a pen out of her pocket and got to work doodling on her arm and shoes.

Justin, who didn't have the attention span to listen to Mr. Whitaker's droning or anything to help keep him entertained, took to scanning the room to see what other people were doing. Three rows in front of him a girl with purple hair was bending an eraser in midair and the two guys next to her were thumb wrestling.

Justin turned his attention to the auditorium. The back of the stage was partially obscured by a large red curtain, the sconces along the wall were lit, though most of the light came from the fluorescents overhead, and the back wall was covered in photos in golden frames.

Justin turned his attention back to Eliza. She had drawn a series of squares on her arm and what looked like a dolphin on her shoe.

"Wow," Justin whispered.

"Thanks," Eliza smiled, glancing up from her drawings.

"And that is why we are still in business," Mr. Whitaker chuckled at the joke no one else had heard.

"Thank you Mr. Whitaker for those guidelines," Miss Andromeda said, moving the microphone stand towards the back of the stage as three other teachers came out from behind the red curtain, two of them carrying a table between them. There was something on the table, but it was covered by a dark blue tablecloth.

"Now, onto the ceremony," Miss Andromeda continued. "If all the first-year students would form a line on the left-hand side of the room," she motioned to her right. "We will begin."

Justin and about twenty other students made their way to the right side, forming a line down the center of the aisle.

Eliza stepped in front of Justin, then turned to give him a cheesily scared face.

Justin laughed silently as she turned back to face the stage.

Miss Andromeda was talking to one of the other teachers, an older woman with long, silvery hair that matched her grey pantsuit. The other two teachers on the stage, both men, were wearing vests and bowties and one of them was holding a yellow towel.

"Welcome first-years," the silver-haired woman said into the microphone. Her voice was crystal clear, like a polished diamond. "My name is Mrs. Strong, I am one of the teachers for the distinct abilities class. We are about to begin with the power revelation ceremony."

Her eyes scanned the line of first-years and seemed to laugh at what they saw.

"Don't worry," she smiled. "It's not hard."

At that moment, Miss Andromeda and one of the male teachers lifted the cloth off the table to reveal five shallow bowls.

"These bowls are each filled with a serum that locates a series of powers within an Ablete," Mrs. Strong continued. "They are organized by how common each ability is by decade, red being the most common, orange the second most, and so on. The blue serum is the rarest, so don't get your hopes up," she smiled knowingly. "The serums are read by a scanner in the bowl that then displays the powers it finds when you stick your finger in it. Now, let's begin."

One of the teachers stepped down from the stage and motioned for the first student in line, a girl with curly, red hair, to join them on stage. He held out a hand for her to take as she climbed the steps and joined the teachers behind the table.

"Thank you, Mr. Wire," Mrs. Strong nodded. "Now dear, what is your name?"

The girl replied, inaudibly to the crowd, and Miss Andromeda wrote it down on her clipboard.

"Now just place your finger in the red serum," Mrs. Strong advised.

The girl stepped forward and carefully dipped her index finger into the potion.

Instantly a red beam shone above the bowl, bearing the words:

"Laser vision: the ability to see through thin objects. May also be able to form laser beams from the eyes. These lasers may or may not cause harm."

A couple of people applauded as the fourth teacher stepped forward and let the girl wipe her finger on the towel.

"And now the orange one…" Mrs. Strong encouraged.

And that's how the ceremony proceeded. The red-headed girl had one red ability, two orange ones, and a pink one. Most kids had a red or orange, maybe a couple of pinks or greens, No one had a blue ability.

After twelve students, it was Eliza's turn.

She mounted the stage looking only the tiniest bit nervous. She stood behind the table, gave Mrs. Strong her name, and drew a deep breath, glaring at the first bowl as she stuck her finger in the serum.

Nothing happened.

Eliza turned around and wiped her finger, not looking the least bit surprised. She turned back to the table and tried the orange one.

Still nothing.

The pink one was the first to reveal an ability and simply read: *telekinesis; the ability to move things with your mind.* The few people paying attention clapped politely as Eliza wiped her finger and moved the next bowl.

The green serum revealed four powers; mind reading, talking through Esp, transformation, and-

"Future seeing," Mrs. Strong read as a hush fell over the room. "We haven't had someone at Capes with that power since me."

Eliza nodded like she knew that's what she'd say.

"Well," Justin thought to himself. *"She might have."*

Thunderous applause broke out in the room, Justin joined in, clapping so hard his hands felt numb by the time the applause stopped.

Eliza tested the blue, then was directed out of the room by Miss Andromeda.

Mr. Wire motioned for Justin to climb the stage. A small tingling rang throughout his chest, growing into a heavy pounding as he faced the crowd of bored students.

"Name?" Mrs. Strong asked, her eyes full of so much kindness that Justin immediately felt calm.

"Justin Strikes."

Miss Andromeda nodded and checked his name off the list.

"Go ahead and try the first serum," Mrs. Strong smiled encouragingly.

Justin drew a shaky breath and stuck a finger into the bright red liquid.

Nothing.

Panic flared in Justin's mind, a wildfire of a thousand voices telling him he was here on accident, that he didn't belong, that there'd been a mistake.

Justin blinked the voices away and turned to wipe his finger on the now splotchy towel.

He turned back to the table and stuck his finger in the orange serum. Immediately a beam shone over the bowls displaying the words: *"Force Fields: the ability to create a shield from energy..."*

Justin let go a breath of relief. He heard Miss Andromeda's pencil scratch against the paper as she wrote something down.

The purply-pink serum read *"telekinesis"* and the green one said *"portal making."*

Justin tried to ignore the distracting buzz of disinterest from the crowd as he stepped closer to the last bowl and stuck his finger in the liquid.

Nothing.

Justin sighed and turned to wipe off his finger, feeling silly for getting his hopes up.

There were gasps from behind him, it sounded like the room itself had released a breath. The teacher holding the towel stood with his mouth agape, his face glowing in blue light.

Justin spun around to read the message displayed above the blue bowl.

"Electric Manipulation: The ability to manipulate or create electricity."

"That power hasn't been seen for thirty years," the teacher with the towel said to Justin. "Congrats! You have a rare gift."

Applause broke out behind Justin, pounding in Justin's ears like the drum of rain against a roof. Miss Andromeda motioned for Justin to join her on the far side of the stage.

"Exit through those doors," she pointed as she continued talking. "Right-hand hall, first room on the left, room 109. You'll get a tour of the school after the ceremony ends." she smiled at him, making her already attractive face light up with pure enthusiasm. "Congrats on the rare ability, I'll see you in Distinct Abilities."

Justin nodded and, praying he wasn't blushing, dismounted the stage.

Room 109

Eliza was at his side as soon as he entered the classroom.

"You got a rare power!" she exclaimed.

Justin nodded as she pulled him into a chair.

"How'd you know?" he asked, scanning the room, expecting to spot a live stream.

"I've been having visions for months now," she tugged on a strand of her hair. "And until I met you, I didn't realize that's what they were, I thought they were just dreams."

"Wow!" Justin nodded. "And yeah, I can control electricity."

"Cool!" she reached into her pocket and pulled out a deck of cards. "Wanna play a game?"

"Sure."

66

Chapter Nine
The Story Set in Motion

Justin, Eliza, and the other first-years waited for the ceremony to end. Eventually, kids stopped entering the room and conversations turned to wonder as everyone waited to see when they'd be collected.

"Is it true you have Electric Manipulation?"

Justin looked up from the card game he and Eliza were playing and saw a sandy-haired kid watching him with wondering eyes.

"Um…" Justin stammered.

"Of course it's true," a thin boy with black hair interrupted. "The serums can't lie. The question is, will the power work? Not everyone with power can use it."

A couple of the kids listening nodded. Justin felt the knot in his stomach grow. Luckily Eliza spoke for him.

"I'm sorry, but who are you?" Eliza scoffed.

"Michael Hunt," he sat up and smiled. "My father works for the government, he's one of the highest-ranking Abletes in the country."

Justin found something weird about the way Michael spoke like a game show host.

"And now, Michael Hunt," Justin thought to himself in a faux announcer voice. *"Son of one of the*

highest-ranking Ablete's in the country. Don't let his cocky attitude fool you, he's probably not as important as he thinks."

A couple of the other kids were nodding in agreement with Michael's statement, the boy with sandy hair was frowning, and Eliza rolled her eyes.

"What-" Justin closed his mouth as the door to the classroom opened.

Everyone was silent as Mrs. Strong stepped into the room. Her pale blue eyes had turned the same silvery color as her hair and were unfocused as they gazed upon the room.

"Mrs. Strong?" asked the girl with curly red hair. *Mary Anne*, Justin recalled one of the girls calling her.

Mrs. Strong turned her face towards her, her eyes still unfocused as she started speaking.

"There was a man who wanted to bring change. He had a vision of a world where all were equal in status," she started pacing the aisles of chairs. "He sought to destroy society and build it his way from the ground up. He gathered large followings who wreaked havoc across the world. He found anyone who opposed him and destroyed them."

Justin felt a shiver go down his spine as if a drop of cold water was running down his shirt.

Mrs. Strong continued her story.

"*Blackglycerin,* as he called himself, unleashed a terror into the world and as terror grew, a group of people rose to stop him. They found his weakness, but he got to them before they could stop him."

She stopped in front of Justin, handheld out in his direction as she addressed him.

"His people are the ones responsible for the attack your parents were in."

Justin sensed the gaze of everyone on him as the teacher continued down the aisle. Eliza scanned his face as his mind flooded with a thousand thoughts. Her face made a sudden change. Her eyebrows scrunched up, her lower lip quivered, and her eyes brimmed with tears, but she turned away before she cried.

Mrs. Strong continued.

"Once he had silenced his enemies, Blackglycerin was ready for the next phase of his plan. However, the quiet was too loud, and people began to take notice. Blackglycerin went into hiding, but soon, his plans will come to fruition. He is hiding here at the school. And it will be up to one of you to stop him."

There was a pause as she left the room. Then the room exploded into chatter.

"Do you wanna talk about it?" Eliza quietly asked, ignoring the others wondering.

"Not yet," Justin replied quietly.

Eliza nodded.

Ten minutes later

"Hi!" Amber said as she entered the room followed by six teachers.

"We have been informed that you have witnessed a 'prophecy,'" said a teacher. Amber frowned slightly as he made air quotes for the word prophecy.

"And we are here to reassure you that the school is still safe," said another.

"Mr. Quakes is right," a different teacher chimed. "There is no undercover villain here."

"Right," Amber said, shaking the frown off her face. "A call will be made to your parents, assuring them that there is nothing to worry about. Now! Who's ready for the tour?"

Five minutes later: main foyer

"This is the main foyer," Amber announced.

"Yeah, no kidding," Eliza muttered. Justin snorted, failing to suppress his laugh.

"Every room on this floor is numbered one hundred," Amber continued. "So if a class on your

70

syllabus is in a room with a one hundred number, it's on this floor. Most of the classes on this floor are ability-centered classes along with a couple of training rooms."

"Training rooms?" someone from the back asked.

Amber nodded. "We have three, each one focused on preventing a certain type of damage. On the second floor are the rooms numbered two hundred, and on the third floor, the rooms labeled three hundred. The fourth floor is the principal's office, along with a couple of teacher's offices and the nurses' wing."

Amber led everyone around the first floor before corralling them outside.

"The building to the left is the girls' dormitory," Amber said, gesturing towards the buildings behind the main one. "And the one to the right is the boys. You'll get a tour of those from your year's dorm monitor, but first, I'm going to show you the rest of campus!"

Amber first showed them the back building, which housed the dining hall/lunchroom, rec room, the library, and the movie room. Next, she took them outside past the field and track areas for P.E. and "other events." Lastly, she showed them the gardens.

"Why do we even have gardens?" Justin asked.

"When the school first opened it was customary for there to be gardens on campus," Amber explained.

"Now it's kind of a tradition to keep the gardens in shape for the newer generations."

She started leading the way back towards the main building.

"Hey," the sandy-haired boy who'd talked to him earlier said, jogging to catch up to Justin. "You're the one she spoke to in the prophecy, right?"

"Ye- Yeah," Justin nodded. "That's me."

"Are you going to try and stop him?"

"I- I don't know. I haven't thought about it," Justin thought for a second. "I don't see why I'd have to."

"What? Do you think the teachers are going to do something about it?" Eliza said, joining their conversation.

"Why not?" Justin replied. "Isn't it their responsibility?"

The other boy shook his head.

"They don't get paid enough," he said. "And even if they did, they might not find him. If they plan on searching for him they won't tell us."

"Why not?" Justin asked.

"They don't want us to think the prophecy was real," he shrugged. "They don't want us worrying about it. But from what I've read, prophecies almost always come true."

"Good to know..." Eliza muttered, messing with the zipper on her jacket.

Justin nodded as the group came to a stop in front of the main building.

"What's your name?" Justin asked.

"Simon," he smiled.

"I'm Justin and this is Eliza."

Eliza smiled and gave a short wave.

"Okay!" Amber called. "We will now be splitting up for the dorm tours. The girls will go with Miss Núñez," she pointed to a woman standing to the left of the group. "And the boys will go with Mr. Franklins."

Justin couldn't see through the group, but he deduced that Mr. Franklins was probably standing somewhere nearby.

Eliza gave him a mock salute and followed the rest of the girls making their way to their dorm.

"Justin," Amber said, motioning for him to stay back. "I need to talk to you for a minute. Mr. Franklins," she called over Justin's head. "I'm borrowing this one real quick!"

She turned back to Justin. "I wanted to make sure that you were okay. I know that my mother spoke to you during the prophecy and something like that can really shake a person up."

"Your mom?" Justin frowned.

"Mrs. Strong," Amber smiled. "She seems to be under the impression that you deserve to know the truth about the prophecy, though I'm not sure why. The prophecy isn't fake. We don't know if you're going to be the one to stop him or not, but my mother has a hunch that you have something to do with this. However, Mr. Whitaker was right in not wanting everyone freaking out, so… be careful who you tell."

"Yeah... I'll- I'll try not to tell anyone who might spill the beans," Justin nodded.

"Wow. I just said 'spill the beans,'" Justin grimaced inwardly. *"I didn't know people said that."*

"Okay, let's get you to the rest of your tour," She smiled. "And remember if something happens, my mom and I are here to help."

Mr. Franklins, a tall man with dark red hair, was waiting for them at the door.

"Mr. Franklins." Amber nodded to Justin. "This is Justin."

"Nice to meet you, Justin!" Mr. Franklins gave him a smile. "I'm going to give you a quick tour of the dorms before we get you settled."

"Okay," Justin nodded.

"The first door here leads to my room," Mr. Franklins pointed to the first door to the right. "I'm the first-year dorm monitor, so if you ever need me that's where I will be. This door," he pointed to the next door on the right, "is your dorm. The last door on the right is the second-year dorm."

They reached the end of the hall. "First door on the left is the common room. There are TVs, couches, and a couple of desks for studying and the next one," he pointed to the next door, "is the bathroom."

"What's that door for?" Justin asked, pointing to the door at the end of the left side hall.

"The glitch room," he held open the door.

"What's a glitch?" Justin asked, studying the white walls and couch in the room.

"A glitch is usually for computers or something when they malfunction. For us, it's when an Ablete over or under uses their powers resulting in something going wrong," Mr. Franklins explained before pointing to the elevator at the end of the hall. "And this is the elevator, it's off-limits to first and second years because your dorms are on this floor, so don't try and use it for joyrides."

"Who would joyride an elevator?" Justin wondered.

"Tonight there's a party to celebrate the beginning of the semester," Mr. Franklins said as they headed back up the hall. "So if you want to change, you can do that now. Your luggage should be in that pile," he pointed to a small pile by the door. "The party's in an hour."

"Justin!" Simon said, waving him over as he entered the dorm. "There's an empty bed next to me!"

Justin smiled, grabbed his bags, and walked over to where he was standing.

"I- I mean…" Simon tried to shrug nonchalantly. "If you want to use the bed next to me. You- You don't have to if you- if you don't want to."

"No," Justin laughed. "That sounds good."

Simon gave him a wide grin.

"Cool…" He nodded. "Did Mr. Franklins tell you about the party?"

Chapter Ten
A Familiar Face

"Who's ready to party!" Amber asked as the first years met in front of the main building.

A couple of people cheered.

"Okay then." Amber laughed. "Let's go!"

She led the way down the cobblestone path between the main building and the girls' dorm. Justin scanned the group for Eliza but stopped when he saw the back lawn.

"Woah," Simon gasped.

The back lawn that they had walked across earlier that afternoon was now lit up by dozens of string lights overhead. The brick patio was being used as a dance floor and was dotted with teens dancing and chatting. Justin spotted a DJ's booth in front of the recreational building and on the grass lawn, were picnic tables decorated with silvery centerpieces, fake candles, and another type of light that reflected red, blue, and green everywhere.

"Yeah, it's cool, isn't it?" said a voice from behind them.

Justin turned to see Eliza wearing a poofy, pink dress.

"Before you say anything, it's not my dress," she scowled. "One of the volunteers misplaced my bag, so I had to borrow some clothes from Lynn Edwards. She told me that I had to wear a dress for the dance."

"Well…" Justin blinked in surprise. "You look nice."

"Thanks, I guess," Eliza said, crossing her arms.

"Anyways-" Justin was interrupted by a voice speaking out of the speakers.

"Welcome everyone," Valerie, the girl Amber had asked for help from, said into the mic at the DJ's table. "I've got a couple of reminders before we start. First off, all students must be accompanied back to the dorms to get pictures taken for this year's I.D.s. Secondly, no one is allowed to use their powers, this includes any seventh-years! Lastly…"

She gave the crowd a mischievous smile.

"Have fun!" she yelled as the DJ started up the music. "Party ends at ten!"

A horde of people headed to the dance floor. Eliza weaved her way through the crowd and sat at one of the tables. Justin glanced at Simon, shrugged, and followed.

"So what are we going to do to find Blackglycerin?" Eliza asked as they sat down.

"I still don't understand why it's up to us," Justin admitted. "Why wasn't anyone able to catch him the first time? I mean... I grew up with Normals, so I don't know this stuff."

"You know how comic book superheroes have secret identities?" Simon asked.

"Yeah," Justin blinked, surprised by the question.

"Well Abletes who attend Ablete schools," Eliza continued. "They're given the option to create new identities when they graduate..."

"So no one knew who Blackglycerin was or where he was from," Simon finished.

"Oh," Justin nodded. "So how are we supposed to find him?"

"We could use our powers," Simon suggested. "Once we've learned how to use them they might be useful."

"Yeah!" Justin nodded enthusiastically. "Eliza, you have mind-reading, that could be useful."

Eliza nodded. "Yeah, I'm just not sure how long it will take for me to be able to use it well... So far it's just kind of a random thing."

"So what should we do until we can use our powers better?" Justin asked.

"We could…" Simon said before stopping abruptly.

"We could what?" Eliza encouraged.

Simon shrugged. "We could make a list of suspects and… and try to figure out who it could be by process of elimination…"

"That's a good idea!" Justin nodded.

"Yeah," Eliza agreed.

"Cool," Simon grinned. "So we have a plan."

There was a silence among the trio as the song ended and another one began.

"So…" Simon said, coughing away the silence. "Wanna dance?"

He froze, eyes wide in panic as he realized he was looking at Eliza.

"I me- I mean… all three of us... As a group."

"Sure, let's dance," Justin stood.

Eliza raised an eyebrow at him, but Justin just raised one of his in return.

"If you can hear this Eliza," Justin thought. *"Just agree with me okay? You can punch me tomorrow, but come have fun with your new friends."*

"Okay, let's dance," Eliza stood. Whether or not she heard his thought was unclear.

Simon gave Justin an incredulous look as they followed Eliza to the edge of the dancefloor.

Eliza, surprisingly, was the first to let loose. Justin and Simon followed her example and song after song, they danced and laughed along to the music. Justin forgot all about being away from home in a world he never knew existed and reveled in the new things he noticed about the people around him; The way Simon snorted when he laughed, the way Amber shouted "This is my song" every two songs, and the way Eliza banged her head to the music were some of the most prominent.

After fifteen songs, the music stopped.

"Imperium!" a boy's voice rang out over the mumblings of the crowd.

"Imperium!" several voices echoed in return.

"Who are we?" asked the first voice.

"Imperium!" the voices replied.

"We are!"

"Power!"

"We are!"

"Imperium!"

Cheers erupted from various spots in the crowd as the chanters fell silent.

"What was that?" Simon asked, trying to peer through the crowded dance floor to see the chanters, who were now gathering in the middle of the dance floor.

"Loud," Eliza frowned.

The crowd began to dissipate as the music started back up, giving the trio a better look at the group and their leader. He was facing away from them but turned around when one of the other boys tackled him from behind.

Justin gasped.

"Do you know him?" Eliza asked, following his gaze.

"That's my brother," Justin gave her an excited smile, which she returned with a look of alarm. "I haven't seen him in months!"

Terrence was mid-laugh when he spotted his brother.

"Justin?" he asked, his hazel eyes widened as Justin made his way towards him. "Hey! I forgot you were here… I didn't make it to the ceremony. How are you, what powers do you have?"

"I'm good," Justin smiled. "And telekinesis, portals… Force fields and Electric manipulation."

"Woah!" said the kid on Terrence's left, an African American boy wearing a bright yellow dress shirt. "Dude, that power is super rare!"

He put forward a fist. Justin nervously tapped it with his own fist.

"Is this your brother?" asked the guy to his right.

"Yep," Terrence nodded. "This is Justin. Justin this is Matt," he jerked his thumb at the guy on his right. "And Peyton."

"Sup," Matt held up his hand in a gang sign as his hair fell into his face.

"Matt, you so look stupid right now," Peyton laughed. "And that's coming from me," he pointed at his shirt.

Matt let loose a barking laugh.

"Nice one." Terrence smirked and turned back to Justin. "I've got a meeting to lead, but I'll talk to you later, okay? Congrats on the rare ability!"

Matt let out a loud whoop as Terrence led the group off the dance floor, leaving Justin alone in their wake.

"Was it just me..." Eliza said as she and Simon approached Justin. "Or did he seem unexcited to see you?"

"I think he was just busy," Simon shrugged. "It probably wasn't personal."

Justin nodded.

"It's nothing I'm not used to," he sighed inwardly.

"I'm going to get some punch," he mumbled, heading off towards the refreshment tables.

"Fruit punch or sparkling cider?" the volunteer asked as he approached the table.

"Punch, please."

She handed him a cup.

"Thank you," Justin said, turning away.

"Clara, why are you still on about this?" asked a voice from nearby.

Justin turned and saw two first-year girls standing at the end of the dessert table.

"Because it matters to me!" the girl in a bright pink dress said angrily. "Some nobody got a rare ability instead of me!"

Justin moved over to the food table, pretending to pick out a cupcake as he listened discreetly.

"But Clara," the girl in a pale blue dress frowned. "Michael said that he might not be able to use the power."

"With my luck, he'll be great at it," Clara mumbled. "And then what am I gonna do Kathryn?"

Justin left before Kathryn could reply.

He made his way back to where Eliza and Simon had last been and found them a couple feet away from the spot. Eliza was jumping along to the music, a song by some band Justin wasn't familiar with, with one of the other first-year girls as Simon awkwardly hopped next to them. Simon waved Justin over when he spotted him.

"How's the punch?" he asked.

"Really sweet," Justin laughed, taking another sip. "I think I'm addicted."

Simon giggled. "I need to get some."

An hour and a half later

"That. Was a lot of fun," Simon declared as he climbed into his bed.

"Yeah," Justin agreed, rubbing at his finger, which had tingled for some reason when his fingerprint was being added to the database. "Not a bad day."

"A great day," Simon supplied.

"Fantastic."

"Amazing."

"Marvelous," Justin smiled as his eyes fell closed.

Chapter Eleven
The First Day of School

Justin woke up with the sun shining in his eyes. He rolled over and saw that Simon was already up and dressed as were a majority of the other boys.

"Am I going to be late?" Justin asked, hurrying to sit up.

"Nah..." Simon looked up, as he finished tying his shoes. "Everyone's up early 'cause they're nervous."

"Oh, okay," Justin nodded.

"Crap!" Justin frowned, pulling a shirt out of one of his drawers. *"Now I'm nervous too."*

Ten minutes later

"Good Morning!" Mr. Franklins said as he entered the room carrying a large cardboard box. "I've got I.D.s and schedules for everyone, but don't come rushing over here just yet!" he laughed as a couple of the boys ran towards him. "I'll call you over here one at a time."

He set down the box and started pulling out badges and calling names. After nine names, he called Justin's.

"Hang on, let me find your schedule," Mr. Franklins said, flipping through a stack of papers. "Strikes, Strikes, Stri... Aha!"

He pulled out a schedule. "Here ya go."

"Thank you," Justin said, taking the I.D. badge and paper from him and looking over the schedule as he walked back to his bed.

Mon. Wed. Fri.

Time	Room	Class
8:00-8:45	302	Telekinesis and Portals
8:50-9:35	104	Ablete Science
9:40-10:25	103	Power Discreteness
10:30-11:15	Back Building	Lunch

****

Justin looked up from his schedule and found Simon standing next to him.

"What classes do you have?" Simon asked.

Justin handed him his schedule.

"We have most of the same classes," Simon said, giving him an excited glance. "I guess that means we have some powers in common. Most people end up having a lot of classes in common anyways, but still... That's cool."

"How do you know all of that?" Justin asked, folding his schedule and putting it in his backpack.

"I ask a lot of questions." Simon shrugged. "Most of them get answers."

"Okay!" Mr. Franklins said as he rose to his feet. "Let's go to the dining hall and get some breakfast!"

At breakfast

"What's ya order?" asked a lady standing next to the line for cereal.

Justin as Simon stared at the stranger in surprise. Unlike the collection of southern accents Capes had, this woman spoke in a slight Scottish accent.

"Carrie you don't even work in the cafeteria," Amber laughed. "The hairnet's a nice touch though."

"I thought you'd like that," Carrie laughed and pulled the fishnet piece out of her strawberry-colored hair as she made her way into the kitchen.

"Who's she?" Justin asked, turning to Simon.

"That's Carrie," Amber said, turning to face them. "She transferred here from Scotland when she was in her seventh year and got a part-time job at a fast-food place in Atlanta. After she graduated Mr. Whitaker hired her to work on the janitorial staff. Now she's head of the janitorial department."

"Oh." Justin nodded. "Cool."

"Yep," Amber smiled. "Good luck on your first day guys!"

"Thanks," Justin smiled as she walked off to join her friends.

"Why does she know so much?" Simon asked.

"Probably has something to do with being a teacher's kid," Justin shrugged as they headed to join the first-year boys at a table.

"Morning," said Eliza as she sat down next to Justin. A couple of the boys gave her a weird look as she sat down.

"What?" she scowled. "Do I have something in my teeth?"

They shook their heads and looked away as they continued with their conversation.

"You have something in your hair though," Justin smirked, pointing to the streak of color.

"Hilarious," Eliza rolled her eyes but was smiling. "Can I see your schedule?"

"MmHmm…" Justin mumbled through his eggs as he pulled it out of his bag.

Eliza scanned the page and compared it with hers.

"Oh cool! We have all but one class together," she said nonchalantly, the glimmer in her eyes betraying her excitement.

"Awesome!" Justin nodded as he took another bite of eggs.

Twenty minutes later

A loud screech rang throughout the cafeteria.

"Sorry, sorry!" a voice said from the P.A. system. "I always forget it does that."

"It's Mr. Whitaker!" Justin realized.

"It's about time for class to start," Mr. Whitaker continued. "Good luck to everyone on the new school year and remember; Scientia sit potentia."

With that, the speakers released another loud crackling sound and shut off. Everyone started standing up and grabbing their bags to head to class.

"We have Telekinesis and Portals first, right?" Simon asked.

"I think so…" Eliza patted her pockets, looking for her schedule.

"We do," Justin confirmed.

"Cool," Eliza nodded, leading their way out of the building.

Three minutes later

Justin wasn't sure what he had expected a class for kids with superpowers to look like but whatever he had pictured, it involved fewer pineapples.

Room 302 was mostly empty aside from a desk and a large bookshelf. The peculiar thing was the array of baseball caps, books, footballs, pineapples, and boxes that were sitting on the shelves.

"Welcome, welcome!" said Mr. Wire, closing the door behind them.

Justin leaned against one of the windowsills and studied his teacher. He was kind of short (something Justin could relate to) and had doused his dark blond hair in hair gel (something Justin couldn't relate to).

"I'm Mr. Wire," he continued. "And, as I'm sure you've guessed, I teach Telekinesis and Portals. We're going to start by breaking up into groups according to what powers you have, so if you only have telekinesis, go stand in a line on the left side of the room."

Three students, including Eliza, made their way towards the left.

"Okay, good," Mr. Wire smiled. "Now, if you only have portals, go stand to the right."

Simon, the blonde girl Justin had overheard at the party, and two other kids headed to the right.

"The rest of you either have both or are in the wrong class," he chuckled to himself. "You can form a line in the middle."

Justin and the three remaining students stepped forward and formed a line.

Mr. Wire smiled, causing creases to form in the corners of his eyes.

"How many of you have been able to use your powers?" he asked. "Specifically telekinesis."

Eliza was the only one to raise a hand. Her eyebrows scrunched together as she turned and scanned the faces of everyone in the room. Justin frowned, trying to recall if telekinesis was the one that let you move things with your mind.

"Mr. Wire," she said, raising an eyebrow at Justin before turning to face the teacher. "Three of them are lying."

"Are they?" he smiled. "Thank you, Miss…"

"Thistle. Eliza Thistle."

"Thank you, Miss Thistle," he gave her a nod before addressing the rest of the room. "If the three of you who are being humble would please raise your hands, it will save us all some time."

Justin hesitantly raised his hand. As did one of the girls in front of him and a boy behind Eliza.

"Good," Mr. Whitaker nodded. "Would any of you like to volunteer? Maybe a boy and a girl…"

"I'll go," Eliza offered.

"Awesome, anyone else?"

Eliza caught Justin's eye, her eyes daring him to volunteer.

"I can go," Justin sighed.

"Thank you," Mr. Wire nodded again. "So, what I'd like for you to do is lift this," He picked a pencil out of the cup on his desk. "Off the desk and levitate it to your hand," he put the pencil down. "Which of you would like to go first?"

"I can," Justin said.

"Great! Come stand here," he pointed to a spot a couple of feet away from his desk. "And what is your name?"

"Justin."

"Okay, Justin," he smiled encouragingly. "Go whenever you're ready."

Justin took a deep breath, gave his head a slight shake to clear his thoughts as he zoned in on the pencil.

Someone coughed from behind him.

"Focus," Justin muttered to himself. He closed his eyes and imagined the pencil flying to him.

Someone gasped.

Justin opened his eyes and saw the pencil floating towards him. Carefully, while trying to keep his focus, Justin held out his hand and grabbed the pencil as light applause filled the room.

"Well done Justin!" Mr. Wire applauded as Justin gave him the pencil. "Now it's Eliza's turn."

Eliza nodded, taking half a step forward. She held out her hand and the pencil shot into the air and landed in her hand with the speed of lightning.

"I see someone has been practicing," Mr. Wire said as she handed the pencil back to him.

"Yeah," Eliza blushed.

"How big of an item can you move?" he asked.

Eliza turned towards the bookshelf and held her hands out towards it. One of the pineapples moved slightly.

Eliza's face hardened into a fierce glare.

The pineapple toppled off the shelf and flew towards Mr. Wire, who caught it with both hands.

"Wow," he nodded.

"That's the largest size I can move," Eliza said, her face flushed.

"That's better than some of my third-year students can do. However, it has probably drained your resources."

Eliza nodded, her face beaded with sweat.

"I think I need to sit down," she muttered, leaning against the desk.

Mr. Wire nodded and pulled the chair out from behind his desk.

"I think it's wise for you to rest for the remainder of our class time," Mr. Wire advised as he ushered Eliza into the chair. "As for the rest of you, I'd like for you to take turns trying to pull an object off of the shelf. Start with the smallest objects and please try not to hit each other. If you feel ready enough, you can try to place a hat on my head. If you only have portals you are welcome to start reading chapter one of your textbooks," he pointed to the books on his desk. "Or you can practice for me. We'll be starting portals on Wednesday."

2nd period

Mr. Wane was writing on the blackboard when they arrived.

"Take care of where you sit," he said as he continued writing. "That will be your seat for the rest of the school year."

Justin, Eliza, and Simon hurried to grab seats in the second row.

"As the board says," Mr. Wane said as the last student sat down. "I am Mr. Wane and today we'll be discussing glitching."

He leaned back against the front of his desk.

"I've always thought it'd be smart to start you first years off with understanding what might happen if you get too cocky and overuse your powers. Though, some of my fourth-year students might need a refresher on this," he sighed. "So, let's get started. Glitches are caused when an Ablete over or under uses their powers. An Ablete's power works kind of like a battery, when you use too much power it causes you to feel drained. However, when you don't use enough power it can overflow into your system, also causing a glitch. Since all of you are still young, your batteries are mostly on the smaller side, meaning you're likely to get drained sooner. As you get older your battery will get bigger and you'll be able to do more with your abilities."

A girl on the front row raised her hand.

"Yes?" Mr. Wane nodded at her.

"Do all powers have the same glitches?"

"Excellent question!" Mr. Wane smiled. "What's your name?"

"Ansleigh Booker, sir."

"Well, Ansleigh, it depends on the ability and its complexity. For example, Telekinesis is a complex ability, so its glitches are more fine-tuned to over and under usage. If you overuse it, you might have a fainting spell, whereas headaches are more common if you underuse it. Since telekinesis is used in the brain, the head suffers during the glitch, whereas a power such as the ability to understand languages would affect the throat because it requires the user to speak."

End of 2nd period

"We have five minutes left before the bell rings," Mr. Wane announced. "So I'm going to hand out these information cards specific to your glitches. When I call your name you can come up to my desk and grab yours."

Justin Strikes

Telekinesis - Blurry vision, fainting spells, headaches (all three are common for both, however, fainting spells are more common for overuse)

Electric Manipulation - Spurts of energy and or electricity (under), Powers not working, draining energy from nearby sources (over)

Force Fields - Randomized shielding (under), defective shields (over)

Portals - Harmful or defective portals (Both)

Justin put down his card and turned to Eliza.

"Yikes! Glitching sounds awful," He winced.

"No kidding!" Simon interjected. "I have vocal manipulation and if I overuse it, I could temporarily lose the ability to talk."

"That's not as bad as mind reading!" Eliza objected, frantically waving her card in their faces. "If I don't read minds often enough I could hear *everyone's* thoughts, whether I want to or not. And with future seeing, I could have an episode and not remember days at a time. It's a nightmare!"

Justin glanced at Simon, who stared wide-eyed at Eliza.

"You win," Justin seceded as the bell rang.

99

Lunch

"What. A. Boring. Class." Justin groaned as he and Simon joined some other first-years at a table.

They'd just gotten out of "power discreteness" (or, as Eliza called it, "common sense class").

"I thought it was interesting," said Kimba as she pulled her hair up.

"It's a useless class," Eliza argued. "Any smart person knows not to reveal their powers to a Normal."

"Exactly," Zachariah agreed. "Just because we're twelve doesn't mean we're stupid."

"Actually over a hundred Abletes accidentally reveal their powers every year," Bailey said. "And at least a quarter of those are kids our age."

"How would you know?" Luke Marsh asked.

"My dad works in cover-ups," she said, tugging on a strand of her hair. "He complains about it a lot."

Justin watched as she stabbed at her fruit salad, more of her blonde curls falling into her face as she took a bite.

Justin realized he was staring and looked down at his food, his face heated like a thawing chimichanga in the microwave.

Thirty minutes later

There were ten minutes left until the end of lunch, Kyle and Annie, the Key twins, were arguing about whether or not some T.V. show was good, and then the room erupted in screams.

"What happened?" called a teacher.

"Someone fainted!" a student yelled. "I think she's dead!"

"She's not dead!" another replied.

Justin stood and tried to see through the cluster of people gathered around the table of screaming teenagers.

"Make way! Make way!" called a woman, as she made her way through the crowd.

"Let her through!" called Mr. Franklins. "She's a doctor."

Justin peered through the crowd to see the doctor kneeling next to a girl in Terrence's grade. The girl seemed to be unconscious, sprawled out on the floor with her strawberry blonde hair spilling out all around her. Most disturbingly, she was shaking slightly, like a rag doll on top of a running washing machine. The doctor leaned forward, gathered her up in her arms, and stood.

"Move!" she yelled. "I've got to get her to the medical bay!"

"We have a medical bay?" Justin asked.

"Weren't you paying attention during the tour?" Simon frowned. "It's on the fourth floor with Mr. Whitaker's office."

Justin nodded as another loud screech came from the P.A. system.

"Attention students," Mr. Whitaker called. "Please make your way to your next class. Your regular schedule will commence as normal."

Protests erupted from the room, but everyone made their way to their next class without much of a fight.

"Wow," Eliza nodded. "That was unfortunate."

Chapter Twelve
Suspects and Subjects

Mr. Franklins was waiting in room 202 as everyone grabbed a seat.

"As you probably know," Mr. Franklins said. "I'm not Miss Brush. She is still out on her lunch break, so I'm here to supervise you until she gets back."

"Well, wait no longer!" said Ms. Brush as she ran into the room. "I am here. Thank you, Mr. Franklins, for watching my class."

"No problem," Mr. Franklins headed for the door. "I now leave them in your capable hands."

"World History!" Ms. Brush said, dropping her bag on her desk. "'In the beginning, God created the heavens and the earth.' Genesis one. That's how Christians believe the world was created. Regardless of your belief, you can't argue that the world came into existence. I won't get into the religious side of history until your fourth year when we'll take a look at different religions through history, so don't argue with me just yet. Sound fair?"

She glanced around the room as everyone nodded in agreement.

"Good," she smiled. "Now, pull out your book and turn to chapter one, page twelve I believe."

Next period

"Distinct Abilities is next," Justin announced as they left History.

"Yes!" Eliza cheered. "I can't wait to see how this class works with so many powers in the class."

"Yeah..." Simon stopped walking. "Tell me how it goes?"

"You're not in that class," Justin stopped next to him.

"Oh," Eliza winced. "Sorry."

"It's okay," Simon shrugged. "I've got a study hall, so I get a head start on homework. I'll see you guys later."

Simon turned and headed upstairs, leaving Justin and Eliza at the bottom of the stairwell.

"We could have handled that better," Justin thought.

"We're going to be late to class if we keep standing here," Eliza said, descending the stairs.

Miss Andromeda was waiting for them when they entered the room.

"Take a seat at the front of the room, we'll get started soon," she said as Justin and Eliza entered the room.

Mrs. Strong was seated behind the desk at the front of the room. She glanced up as more students came in and continued checking boxes off on the attendance sheet in front of her.

"Welcome to Distinct Abilities, everyone!" Miss Andromeda said, shutting the classroom door behind the last student. "We have a lot of powers represented here, so for this first semester, we'll be splitting into two groups each week to try and cover all the abilities. This way, each person gets a chance to learn about their abilities, as well as a majority of the other powers represented here."

"What if your power isn't one of the ones being discussed this week?" asked Michael.

"Then you'll still be expected to be here," Mrs. Strong said. "Not everyone has the opportunity to take this class because not everyone has a rare enough ability. So consider it a privilege."

Michael nodded seriously, leaning back in his chair.

"Group one," Miss Andromeda continued. "Bailey, Michael, Luke, Abigail, Kimba, Justin, and Eliza, will be with me in the back of the room."

"Everyone else is with me," Mrs. Strong said.

Miss Andromeda made her way to the back of the room, motioning for them to follow.

"Grab a chair, make a circle, and we'll begin," she said, picking up one of the grey, plastic chairs and moving it by the window.

"Wow, this chair is heavy," Justin thought to himself. *"Or maybe I'm just weak… No, the chair's heavy."*

Eliza smirked as she set her chair down.

"Today we'll be starting with Weather Manipulation," Miss Andromeda said as everyone settled into their seats. "Two of you have that ability; Bailey and Kimba."

Both girls nodded.

"Have either of you been able to use it?" Miss Andromeda asked.

Bailey nodded, while Kimba shook her head.

"Kimba, we'll work on your ability to use it," she nodded kindly. "A lot of people aren't able to use an ability on the first try, especially when they don't know what they're trying to do."

She turned to Bailey. "Do you think you would be able to demonstrate for the group?"

Bailey nodded, took a deep breath, and looked up at the ceiling. Justin noticed her scrunch up her nose in concentration and suppressed a smile.

Dark, wispy clouds formed underneath the fluorescent lights. Everyone, including the other group, stared in amazement as the wisps joined together and became more cloudlike. Then it started to pour, dousing the room in rain. There was a roll of thunder and someone, one of the boys, screamed.

"Sorry!" Bailey gasped as the clouds and rain water disappeared. "I'm not good at controlling it."

"Well, that's part of my job," Miss Andromeda laughed. "The main trick to mastering weather manipulation is to keep your mind clear of emotions. Weather manipulation and other manipulation powers; Weather, vocal, and electric manipulation…"

Justin leaned forward in his seat.

"Are all based on emotions. My brother, Ryan, has weather manipulation and when he was younger he would create a small thunderstorm in the kitchen when he was mad and it would rain in the living room when he was upset. The key to defeating a manipulator is to mess with their emotions, making them confused. Now Kimba, let's focus on an emotion and see if we can make it rain again."

End of period

"I hope one of my powers is next," Eliza said, bouncing on her toes as they waited for the bell to ring.

"Me too," Justin nodded. "What class is next?"

"I have Minds next," Eliza said, fiddling with the strap in her bag.

"Oh," Justin pulled his schedule out of his pocket and scanned it. "I have Force Fields. Room 309."

"I have to go to room 301," Eliza said, mounting the first flight of stairs.

Justin followed, racing to keep up with her as she took two steps at a time.

"I've heard a couple of older students say that Mind's a good class," Eliza said, mounting the stairs to the third floor. "I've also heard some people say the Force Fields teacher is one of the best teachers at Capes."

Justin didn't reply. Instead, he worried that he wouldn't like Force Fields. Or wouldn't be good at it. Or that there wouldn't be anyone he knew in the class.

Eliza looked down the hall as they reached the third floor. "I'll see you in Spanish."

"See you in Spanish," Justin said, heading towards room 309.

He entered the room and let go a silent sigh of relief when he realized he knew everyone. Then Justin noticed a new problem.

The desks were two-seaters and all but two of the desks were full. One of them was empty, and Bailey sat at the other.

"I don't want to offend Bailey," Justin thought. *"But I feel weird sitting next to a girl I don't know."*

"Justin," Bailey waved shyly. "You can sit here if you want. I don't bite."

"Thanks," he smiled and he sat next to her, trying to ignore the fluttering feeling in his stomach.

"Welcome everyone!" Miss Drills said, turning away from the blackboard. "I'm Samantha Drills, feel free to call me Samantha or Miss Drills, I'm okay with either as long as you're respectful to the fact that I'm your teacher. Sound fair?"

There were nods and a couple of yeses from the class.

"Awesome!" she smiled. "Now, force fields are a lot more complicated than you'd think. They can be hard to form because they might have holes or be too thin. Even a shield that looks perfect might not be able to withstand an attack for long."

"Why?" Bailey asked.

"Did Mr. Wane explain the battery thing to you?"

"Yeah," The class nodded.

"Well because you guys are young, the shields you form might not be complete," Miss Drills explained. "Force fields need a lot of power to be extremely sturdy, and because your batteries are small, not many first-years can form a shield like that without glitching like crazy. But, that doesn't mean you can't practice!"

She picked up a basket full of apples from behind her desk.

"I'm going to give each of you an apple and I want you to try and form a shield over your apple."

"How?" asked Kyle Keys.

"Picture a force field in your mind, imagine a thin curtain being pulled down over the apple," she started placing apples in front of the students. "It might not be perfect on the first try, but that's why we practice."

"Can we eat the apples?" asked Luke.

"If you can form a shield of any kind over your apple, you may eat your apple."

She placed the basket on her desk. "Remember, a little focus can go a long way."

She stretched her hand towards the basket. A green translucent shield formed over the basket and disappeared with a wave of Miss Drill's hand.

Justin looked down at his apple and tried to focus, but the sound of someone's fingers beating on the table and the feeling of Miss Drills watching them made it hard.

"Yes!" cried Bailey. Justin looked over at her apple and saw a thin, purple shield forming over her apple. There were a couple of holes the size of corn kernels, but other than that it looked perfect.

"Nice, Bailey!" Justin congratulated.

"Excellent!" Miss Drill said, walking over to their table. "Now try and deepen the shade of purple, sometimes first-years are able to strengthen their shield by focusing on darkening the color."

"Okay." Bailey nodded, face scrunched up in concentration.

Justin turned his attention back to his apple.

"Okay Justin, you've got this," he thought to himself. *"Just a nice shield with no holes... maybe one or two holes...."*

Gradually, a blue shield formed over the apple, creeping down the sides of the apple before stopping at the desktop.

"Wow, nice job!" Miss Drills said, looking over from where she stood in front of Bailey. "What's your name?"

"Justin."

"Nice job, Justin," she looked up to address the rest of the class. "If you'd like to take a look at Justin's shield, you can see a good example of a sturdy first-year shield."

Justin tried to keep his blushing to a minimum as everyone looked his way.

"Not many students can produce a shield like this on their first couple tries. But, since we have a shield like this…" she turned and picked up a pencil off of her desk. "I'd like to demonstrate something," she turned to Justin. "May I?"

"Um… Sure!" Justin squeaked, his face burning hotter in embarrassment.

Miss Drills took the pencil and poked the shield. The shield trembled at the touch but didn't break.

"Take a note of that," Miss Drills said, once again addressing the room. "When I poked the shield, it drew Justin's attention away from the shield and to the pencil."

POW! She stabbed the shield so quickly that Justin's attention broke and the shield popped.

"When an Ablete masters using force fields," she continued. "They require less focus to produce one. But for the first couple of years, it can take a while to produce a perfect shield, let alone to do it with little focus. Now," she clapped her hands together. "Let's get back to practicing!"

End of 7th period

"How did you get your force field like that?" Mary Anne asked as they made their way to Spanish.

"I don't know," Justin smiled. "It was just… luck I guess."

"I need luck like that," Luke frowned. "My shield had a bunch of holes."

"If you hadn't poked it so much…" Kyle joked.

"I didn't poke it *that* much," Luke grumbled.

"Hey!" Simon said as Justin entered the Spanish room.

"Hey," Justin said.

"Have you seen Eliza?" Simon asked as Justin sat down next to him.

Justin shook his head. "Not since the beginning of last period."

"Well don't worry, I'm here," Eliza said sitting next to Simon. "Minds ran late. Mr. Fields was thinking of a color and we had to read his mind and say the color. Those of us who *could* read his mind couldn't pronounce it. It was 'coquelicot.'"

"Wait," Justin frowned. "I thought mind reading was like hearing someone's thoughts."

"Sometimes it works like that and other times it's like reading a book. It depends on who's mind you're reading," she shrugged.

"¡Hola Estudiantes!" Miss Núñez said as the last of the students came in. "Let's get started with some Spanish songs."

"Excellente," Eliza muttered.

"Miss Núñez?" Justin said, raising his hand. "Eliza would like to volunteer to sing the first song."

Simon giggled as Eliza gave him a dirty look.

"I'll get you for this, Strikes," she vowed.

Study hall

"Could one of you take these to Mr. Whitaker's office?" Mrs. Rodriguez asked, holding up a couple of forms.

"I can," Simon offered.

"Do you know where it is?" she asked, handing him the papers.

"Fourth floor?"

"That's the one," the teacher smiled.

114

Justin looked over at Eliza. She was hunched over a notebook, making a list of names.

"What's the list for?" he asked, leaning closer.

"Suspects," she whispered.

Justin scanned the list and giggled. "Mr. Goo-bo-goo?"

"That's how it's pronounced," Eliza shrugged. "It's not a full list, obviously, but it's the teachers I have and the staff I could remember."

"I have Ms. Drills for Force Fields," Justin added.

Eliza nodded and put the name on the list.

"Do you want to go to the library after club sign-ups to try and narrow down the suspects?" she asked as the bell rang.

"Sure," he shrugged.

"Mrs. Rodriguez," Eliza said as she packed up her bag. "Would you tell Simon to meet us in the library when he gets back?"

"I'll make sure to tell him," Mrs. Rodriguez smiled.

"Thank you!" Eliza smiled, grabbing her bag and bouncing out of the room.

"Do you know what clubs there will be?" Justin asked, following her downstairs.

"There's art and drama, but other than that I don't know," she shrugged.

Justin froze at the bottom of the stairs. The main foyer was filled to the brim with students waiting in line for club sign-ups.

"Rush hour," Eliza whispered. Her eyes glittered excitedly.

"All first and second years to the left," Miss Andromeda's voice called through a megaphone. "Third, fourth, and fifth years in the middle. Sixth and seventh years to the right."

Justin stepped off the bottom step and made his way through the traffic of the main foyer, Eliza right behind him.

Twenty minutes later

"Hello! First-years?" asked the teacher behind the sign-up desk. His nametag read Mr. Silver.

"Yes," Justin and Eliza said in unison.

"Okay," Mr. Silver nodded, checking his clipboard. "Y'all can take Suit Design, Book Club, or Ways of Deduction on Tuesday and Art or Team Sports on Thursday, or Theatre and Drama on both."

"I'd like to take Art," Eliza said quickly.

"Me too," Justin nodded.

Mr. Silver had them add their names to the sign-up sheet.

"And for Tuesday?" he asked.

"The… deduction one?" Justin offered.

"Yeah," Eliza nodded.

"Okay," he had them sign another sheet. "You two are free to go, enjoy your afternoon!"

Chapter Thirteen
Gathering Wits

"Woah," Justin said as they entered the library. "I forgot how big it was in here."

The library at Capes was huge, taking up most of the second floor. Even for a private school, it was ginormous. Justin scanned the room. There were three tables in the one spot that wasn't taken up by aisles of bookshelves and the room's walls were painted such a faint shade of lavender that they passed for white, which tripped Justin out for a minute, literally since he was so busy staring at the walls that he tripped on a rug.

Eliza was nice enough to pretend she didn't notice. Instead, she made her way to one of the tables and dropped her stuff in a chair.

"I need to finish the list of teachers and staff..." Eliza said, sitting in the chair next to her stuff. "Then we could start investigating and crossing names off the list."

"Start investigating..." Justin nodded. "What if the teachers are doing their own investigation?"

"Then we do our best to not get in their way," she shrugged.

Justin nodded again. "Who's missing from the list?"

"A couple of teachers and a majority of the staff," Eliza scanned her list. "Oh! I forgot to add Mr. Whitaker."

She grabbed a pen and scribbled the name on the top of the page as Simon entered the room.

"Please tell me you signed up for 'Ways of Deduction,'" Simon said, plopping into the chair beside Justin. "I don't want to be alone in a club I don't know anything about."

"We're both signed up for it," Justin assured him.

"It's kind of like a detective's club," Eliza explained. "They teach us how to figure things out with minimal information."

"Oh," Simon nodded. "So what are we working on?"

"A list of everyone who works at Capes," Justin explained.

"Did you put Valerie on the list?" Simon asked.

"No," Eliza looked up from the list. "Why? What does she do?"

"She's Mr. Whitaker's secretary…" Simon made a face. "Or administrative assistant… Something like that."

"Ah," Eliza nodded, adding her name to the list.

"Maybe we can ask someone for a list," Simon suggested.

"Like who?" Justin asked.

Simon looked thoughtful.

"Maybe one of the older students," he shrugged.

"I could ask my sister…" Eliza grimaced. "Nevermind, I'd rather not have to talk to her."

"I could ask Terrence," Justin offered. "He might help."

"Cool," Simon grinned. "So what's next?"

"Figuring out who's not a suspect," Eliza shrugged.

"How do we do that?" Justin asked.

"Well, we can cross Mrs. Strong off of the list," said Eliza.

"Why's that?" asked Justin. "I mean, I like Mrs. Strong, but don't we need proof before we cross someone off the list?"

"Prophecy givers can't be a part of the prophecies they give," Eliza replied. "Visions can involve the seer, but prophecies can't."

"What's the difference?" Justin frowned.

"Prophecies are spoken, Visions are seen."

"How do you know all of that?" Simon asked.

"Mrs. Strong had Amber give me a book about future seers," Eliza shrugged. "I got bored last night, so I read some of it."

"So how do we figure out who else isn't a suspect?" Justin asked as Eliza crossed Mrs. Strong's name off the list.

"Well, until we can use our powers," Simon leaned forward, his elbow resting against the table. "We can try and investigate the teachers and staff… You know, watching them to see if they do anything suspicious. If we're lucky, we'll be able to shorten the list."

"Sounds like a plan," smiled Eliza.

Dinner: cafeteria

"Where did you go after ninth period?" Annie asked Eliza.

"Justin, Simon, and I went to the library," Eliza stabbed her meatloaf.

"What did y'all do at the library?" Bailey asked.

Eliza filled her cheeks with air, released the breath, and shrugged. "We wanted to check out the graphic novels. They have a good selection."

"Awesome!" Annie smiled. "I love graphic novels!"

She looked down the table at her twin. "Kyle! They've got manga in the library!"

"Cool," Kyle nodded.

"Justin," Simon poked him. "There's Terrence."

Justin turned. Terrence was a table away from them.

"I'll be right back," he announced to no one in particular as he pushed his chair back.

The thirty-second walk to Terrence's table was too long for Justin's liking. With each step, another thought rose in his head.

"Should I just ask?" Justin wondered. *"What if he doesn't help? Should I introduce myself to the table?"*

"Terrence!" he said as he walked up to the table.

Terrence glanced up.

"Oh, hey! How was your first day?" he asked.

One of the boys at the table laughed at something one of the girls had said.

"Good," Justin watched the girl next to Terrence try to steal his cornbread.

"Oh my gosh, just take it already, Tammi," Terrence laughed. He dropped the cornbread on her plate.

"So, what's up Justin?" he asked, turning back to face his little brother.

"I was wondering if you could help me make a list of the staff." Justin said.

The girl, Tammi, snorted.

"Who do you think he is?" she laughed. "Raymond Kindle?"

"Who?" Justin frowned.

"A seventh year," Terrence explained. "He's kind of a goody-two-shoes."

"Kind of?" Tammi smirked.

"If you're looking for a list of the staff here," Terrence said, spearing a pea with his fork. "Ask him. He's really into acts of service and gratitude, so he knows each staff member by name."

"Oh," Justin frowned. "Okay… Cool."

Terrence turned back to Tammi and started asking her something.

"Did he help?" Simon asked as Justin sat back down.

"Kind of."

Raymond frowned again, studying him. Then he straightened and held open the door.

"Come on in, Justin."

His dorm was smaller than the first years with just enough room for two beds, a dresser, and a couple of very cluttered desks. Raymond opened one of the desk drawers and started rummaging through it.

"So what do you need the list for?" he asked, pulling out one of the papers.

"We're- I'm..." Justin raced for a lie as Raymond put the paper back into the drawer. "I wanted to make cards for all of the staff... You know, for holidays."

Raymond nodded as he pulled a piece of paper out of the drawer.

"I started keeping lists in my second year," he picked up a pen from his desk and started copying the list onto a blank sheet of paper. "I wanted to be able to pray for each of the staff by name."

"Oh," Justin instantly hated how surprised he sounded.

"I know," he laughed. "I don't seem very religious. So, the list should include everyone. I always ask someone on staff if anyone was added to staff on orientation day. As far as I know, no new staff was hired this year."

He stopped writing and compared the two lists.

"So what's it like to have Terrence as a brother?" he asked, beginning to write again.

"Fine, I guess," Justin shrugged. "I haven't really seen him since he came here, except for a couple of holidays and summers."

Raymond glanced up at him. Justin shifted on his feet uncomfortably.

"Yeah, a lot of students do that," Raymond said, turning back to his writing. "I'm sorry."

"It's okay," Justin shrugged again. "It's not like he abandoned me."

Raymond nodded, putting down the pen.

"Here you go," he held out the copied list. "A complete list of the employees at Capsburg Ablete Power Enforced School."

"Thanks," Justin said, taking the paper from him. "I'll make sure to add Raymond Kindle to our card list."

"Call me Ray," he smiled. "And no problem."

Justin almost turned to leave, but a question rose from the back of his mind.

"Have you heard anything about the girl who passed out at lunch today?"

Ray did a good job hiding his surprise, if he had any.

"Don't repeat this to anyone," Ray warned. "But the doctors think she was poisoned. They're not sure whether it's food poisoning or intentional, they're running some tests, but they agree that the cause isn't natural."

Justin shakily nodded.

"I won't tell anyone," he promised.

Chapter Fourteen
Another Class, Another Suspect

Justin had a text from Mrs. Willows when he woke up.

Just checking to make sure everything's going well. If you want, you can visit your grandfather this Saturday. Just let me know!

Justin smiled and typed his reply.

everythings good. id like to visit

"Do you think they'll have waffles this morning?" he whispered to a stirring Simon.

"They'd better," Simon mumbled.

Third period

"Welcome to History of Heroes!" Mr. Franklins smiled as everyone entered the room. "If you could all direct your attention to me, we'll get started."

"Some Abletes believe that we got our powers as a blessing from God," Mr. Franklins said, flipping through a book. "That is a myth. It is most likely that Abletes got their powers through a type of evolution; as the power was needed, the ability would grow in an Ablete. These abilities might not have been as fine-tuned as ours are today…"

Justin's phone vibrated in his pocket, giving him a mini heart attack. As stealthily as possible, he fished his phone out of his pocket and checked it.

Mrs. Willows: Go to the principal's office sometime today and tell him that you want to visit Martin Lains. They'll contact him and make arrangements for you to visit.

okay, Justin replied.

"Justin," Mr. Franklins said in a stern tone. "Focus please."

Justin gave him a sheepish smile as the class snickered. Mr. Franklins gave him a subtle wink.

"Because these abilities have changed so much, most of our older stories about heroes are more myth than fact. Nonetheless, I'd like to spend a semester talking about these tales of Abletes from all around the world..."

Seventh period: study hall

Justin pulled the list of suspects out of his backpack.

"Who should we investigate first?" he asked.

"The doctors," Simon suggested. "Or the medical staff."

"Why them?" Eliza frowned.

"They're the people we'll see the least," Simon shrugged. "We see teachers in class and kitchen staff during meals, so between the maintenance staff and the doctors, we have a good number of people who are relatively hidden from us. They wouldn't have a hard time hiding something."

"How are we going to investigate them?" Justin asked.

"We buy fake glasses for disguises and follow them!" suggested Eliza.

"We can keep an eye on them, then ask them a question and see if they lie," Simon said, ignoring Eliza's laughs. "If their pupils get big, we'll ask them if they know anything about Blackglycerin. Then, if their pupils get small, we know that they're not in on it."

"And if they're not in on it?" Asked Eliza.

"Then we ask them to help us," Justin offered. "Or not…"

"I think we should keep our investigation a secret," Simon said. "That way, no one else has the information we've gathered. Also, we'll be safer. You know, in case Balckglycerin tries to find us."

"Yeah," Justin agreed. "It'll make it harder for him to find us if we keep it a secret."

"So we keep it a secret?" Eliza said, leaning forward.

"Deal," Justin and Simon said.

Eighth period

Mr. Crain was old. Not on-the-verge-of-death old, but the kind that you could see by the wrinkles around his eyes. His withered face and hands were riddled with scars. His suit was the color of paper bags people used for lunch sacks and was just as wrinkled.

"We live in a world of good and evil," he said in a low tone. "So much of each that we separated our villain and hero histories into two different classes. I like to use the first class of the year to talk and answer questions. So… Anything you want to know?"

Everyone raised their hands so fast, Justin could feel a breeze.

"How about you?" he said, pointing to Jerry Daniels

"Can you tell us about Blackglycerin?"

"Black. Glisser. In..." Mr. Crain nodded as he over-pronounced the name. "An interesting story. No one knows who he really was, only what he did. Blackglycerin craved to change how the equality of the world worked. He gathered forces, forces that caused chaos. They set buildings on fires, planted bombs, and threatened large companies with genocide. As more attacks happened, Blackglycerin himself made more appearances. The Ablete community recognized some of his followers as their fellow Abletes, the circumstances were too much of a coincidence for them to ignore. Eventually, an Ablete safety organization tried to investigate Blackglycerin and his weaknesses. They were able to discover that he had been in an accident, one that left him heavily scarred." he laughed, gesturing to his scars. "Not unlike myself."

There were titters from some of the students. Mr. Crain stopped laughing, his eyes somber.

"They also discovered that his face was marred with what we assume are black birthmarks. This, combined with the bombings earned him the name 'Blackglycerin.' Eventually, Blackglycerin got word that there were people trying to stop him so he attacked."

Justin felt a shiver, like someone had dropped an ice cube down his shirt.

"Some of the people died," Mr. Crain continued. "Others lived, but not as their former selves."

"What do you mean they didn't live as their former selves?" asked Michael.

Mr. Crain paused, his eyes finding Justin's before he continued.

"They live… But they don't remember who they are. Some cases have gaps in their memory, others suffer from PTSD, while others act child-like."

Justin nodded stiffly.

"I myself never got the chance to meet these heroes," Mr. Crain said, sitting on his desk. "However, Mrs. Strong had the pleasure of teaching some of them. In fact, she taught a majority of your parents."

Justin's hand was in the air before he even contemplated raising it.

"Yes?" Mr. Crain blinked in surprise.

"Did she teach my parents?" Justin asked, his heart pounding like a sledgehammer against his chest.

"She did," Mr. Crain nodded.

Justin nodded numbly.

"Cool."

Clubs: ways of deduction

Mr. Johnson was very smiley for someone facing a room of twenty-two students alone.

"Observation is a key skill in an Ablete's life," he placed a bright orange hat on his head. "For those who go into hero work need to have a keen enough eye to find clues that could help them take down a villain. For example, you wouldn't miss me wearing this hat. However, I doubt you noticed the color of my watch… And now you're noticing that I'm not wearing one."

Justin smiled.

"This week I'm going to distribute some peculiar items to different members of staff," Mr. Johnson continued. "It'll be your job to take notice of that person and see how much you remember next Wednesday. Now!" he clapped loudly. "Today, let's see how much you've remembered from today…"

End of clubs

"Wow," Justin giggled. "We are bad at remembering things."

"Speak for yourself," Simon laughed. "I remembered at least half of them."

"That's a lie," Eliza smirked.

"Oh, whatever," Simon smiled. "Wanna head to the sickbay and investigate the nurses?"

"I can't," Justin said, stopping to stand in the hallway. "I have to head to Mr. Whitaker's office and schedule a visit with my grandfather. I don't know how long it'll take."

"Oh," Simon nodded, obviously disappointed that he wouldn't be catching a bad guy today. "Maybe tomorrow during study hall then?"

"Sure," Justin shrugged. "Eliza?"

"Works for me," she nodded.

"Cool," Justin nodded. "I'll see you at dinner."

With that, he turned and headed upstairs to the fourth floor.

"Wait," Justin realized as he emerged from the stairwell. *"Which one is his office?"*

"Looking for something?" asked a voice to his right.

Justin turned to Miss Andromeda standing in one of the doorways.

"Um…" he felt his face grow red. "I need to find Mr. Whitaker's office."

She smiled sweetly.

"Valerie's office is the first on the left down that hall," she pointed down the hall in front of them. "You have to go through her office to get to his."

Justin nodded. "Thank you."

He hurried down the hall.

Valerie looked up as he walked in.

"Hey, how can I help you?" she asked, giving him a small smile.

"I need to schedule a visit with my grandfather," Justin said.

Valerie nodded and opened a new tab on her computer.

"Can do, take a seat."

Chapter Fifteen

Testing the Doctors

Wednesday

Sixth period, Mrs. Strong had talked about the power of "otherseeing," the ability to see things that happen in other places without being there.

Michael was the only one with power and looked extremely proud as Mrs. Strong talked about how the power would develop and what Michael would one day be able to do.

Justin hesitated as he reached the door, deciding to stay behind after the bell rang. Eliza gave him a quizzical look, but after a gesture from Justin, left without him.

"Mrs. Strong?" he asked the last of the first-years left.

"Yes, dear," she looked up from her work.

Justin took a deep breath, letting the cool air fill his lungs as he debated how to phrase the question.

"Mr. Crain said you knew my parents..."

"I did," she smiled mournfully. "Your mother was in this class years ago."

Justin held his breath, waiting for her to continue, scared of what she might not say.

"Her father, your grandfather, had attended Capes when I was in school, though he wasn't in my year. He was quiet, but everyone knew he was a genius. When Clarissa became my student, I saw great potential in her. She was bright for her age. That combined with her superspeed made her a bit of a wild card."

She looked up at Justin and smiled. "I see the same potential in you. Like a flame that could either light up a room… Or burn it down."

Justin felt an ominous chill enter the room but simply nodded as Mrs. Strong continued.

"Your dad I didn't *technically* have in my class," she laughed lightly. "He would sneak in and try to sit next to your mother. He ended up getting some of the best grades in the class. He loved learning and I think he would've made a great teacher."

She looked past him at the rest of the class.

"Speaking of which, I have a class to teach."

"Oh, right," Justin nodded.

"If you want, I could pull out some of my old files and notes and tell you more about your parents."

"I'd like that," he nodded. "Thank you, Mrs. Strong."

"Anytime," she bowed her head slightly. "Now run along, you're going to be late to class."

Study hall

"Mrs. Rodriguez?" Simon said as the clock read three forty-five. "I don't feel good."

Mrs. Rodriguez's head snapped up, her eyes electrified with panic.

"Do you need to go to the nurses?" she asked.

"Justin and I can take him!" Eliza offered as Simon feigned queasiness.

Mrs. Rodriguez nodded.

"That sounds smart," she eyed Simon nervously.

Eliza nodded seriously, leading Simon out of the room as he faked another groan. She gave Justin a triumphant look as they hurried down the hall.

"That was too easy," Eliza whispered as they climbed the stairs.

"All thanks to my acting," Simon said, stopping at the top of the stairs to bow.

"Yes, yes, you did great," Justin laughed. "Don't get a big head about it."

"Too late. I can already feel the swelling," Simon put a hand to his forehead. "We should get me to nurse A-Sap."

"What if we wait to see if your head explodes?" Eliza suggested.

"What if we don't!" Simon said, dashing up the last flight of stairs.

"You can't threaten people's heads," Justin jokingly scolded.

"You can't tell me what to do," she smirked, chasing after Simon.

"How can I help you?" asked the nurse behind the glass of the nurse's station.

"Hi… Martin," Eliza nodded at his nametag. "Simon here has a stomach ache of some kind."

Martin nodded and pressed a button on the intercom.

"Stephanie?" his voice rang out from down the hall as he spoke into the microphone. "There's a kid here with a stomach ache."

"On my way!" a voice called from down the hall.

A blonde woman in green scrubs rounded the corner.

"You three can follow me."

Examination room

"There's no nausea or bloating," Simon said as Stephanie pulled out a clipboard. "And I haven't had any other stomach problems, I'm just crampy."

Justin and Eliza shared a surprised look.

"Wow, Simon thought this through a lot more than we did," Justin thought to himself.

"I doubt it's anything serious," Stephanie nodded. "It's most likely your stomach reacting to something you ate, I can get you some pills for the pain if you want."

"Do you have anything all-natural?" Simon asked. "I don't wanna take anything I'm not supposed to."

"Sure," Stephanie opened the examination room door. "I'll go find something."

"All-natural won't mess up my body," Simon explained as soon as she was out of earshot. "Since I'm not experiencing any actual pain, it's safer."

"Smart," Justin nodded.

"What if she doesn't do anything suspicious we can confront her on?" asked Eliza, keeping an eye on the door.

"We come back and try again," Simon shrugged.

Justin nodded in agreement but mentally began to form a new plan in his head so that next time they'd be better prepared.

Stephanie reentered the room, a small bottle clutched in her left hand.

"It's an essential oil," she said, handing the bottle to Simon. "A couple drops rubbed on your stomach should ease the pain. If you still have pain in an hour, come back and I'll get you something stronger."

Thursday: breakfast

Justin was pouring milk into his cereal when a yell from across the room made him jump and spill milk on the table.

"Help!" called one of the students. "She's been poisoned!"

One of the teachers made their way towards their table and helped one of the students stand to their feet. Justin watched them make their way out of the dining room as he joined his friends at a table.

"Do you think she was really poisoned?" Bailey fretted.

"Yes," Justin thought to himself.

"No," He said aloud.

"It was probably just an allergic reaction to something in the eggs," Eliza shrugged.

"For some reason, I doubt that," Simon muttered.

Justin nodded, an idea popping into his head.

Nurses' wing: later that day

Justin waited in the examination room for Martin to return with bandages. He was fine, he had just drawn on his arm with a red pen to make it look like he'd gotten a scratch. To further sell the effect, Eliza has covered the mark in a mix of red-brown and blood-red paints. Martin had wiped off the paint, assuming it was real blood, seen the "scratch," and left to get bandages for it.

Martin re-entered the room with a roll of white bandages.

"Hold out your arm, please," he instructed.

Justin did as told and watched as Martin started wrapping his arm in white gauze.

"I'm going to have to have a talk to you kids about sword fighting with palette knives," Martin said wearily.

"Could've been worse," Justin shrugged, careful to not move his arm. "There could have been more people hurt."

144

Martin smiled.

"Do you…" Justin paused as Martin finished wrapping his arm. "Do you think someone's poisoning students?"

Martin's head snapped up in surprise.

"What made you think that?" he asked, looking away from Justin.

"Two kids passed out in the first week of school?" Justin frowned exaggeratedly. "It couldn't be anything else… My god mom says I have an overactive imagination." he shrugged.

Martin relaxed.

"It's not poison," he gave Justin a reassuring look, but his pupils had expanded.

"He's lying," Justin noted.

"Do you like being a nurse?" Justin asked, picking at his bandages.

"Yes," he smiled fondly. "It's rewarding to get to help people. Don't pick at your bandages."

"Sorry," he nodded. "Do you know anything about Blackglycerin?"

Justin held his breath as Martin frowned.

"Not really. I was alive during his reign of terror, but I was too young to remember all the details of what happened."

Justin stood to leave.

"Cool, thanks!" Martin's pupils had remained dilated, he didn't know anything about Blackglycerin.

"You're welcome!" Martin smiled as Justin ran out the door. "Don't play with any more sharp objects!"

"Martin doesn't know anything about Blackglycerin," Justin announced as he met Eliza and Simon in the library.

"That's one down…" Eliza crossed his name off the list. "And *a lot* to go."

"I can go tomorrow during study hall," Simon volunteered. "To investigate Stephanie."

"Maybe I should go," Eliza made a face. "They might get suspicious if you're in the sickbay too often."

"It's only my second time," Simon rationalized. "You can go next time."

"Okay," Eliza shrugged. "But if you get questioned, *don't* mention me."

"You can blame it on me," Justin offered. "Just in case they get suspicious."

"We're twelve," Simon rolled his eyes. "They're not going to suspect us of anything except for stealing lollipops."

"They have lollipops?" Eliza frowned.

Chapter Sixteen
A Visit with Grandpa

Saturday

Ms. Núñez came to collect Justin as soon as he was done with breakfast. He said a quick goodbye to Eliza and Simon and followed her to where her car was waiting.

"Normally, Mr. Fields deals with student transportation," Ms. Núñez explained as they pulled out of the Capes driveway. "But he had plans today. Are you excited to see your grandfather?"

"Yeah!" Justin nodded. "I usually only get to see him during the summer or for Christmas."

Ms. Núñez smiled as she turned the car into downtown Arenthia, an Ablete town. "Is he your mom's or your dad's dad?"

"My mom's. Grandpa Strikes died when Terrence was two. I never got to meet him."

"That's what happened with my grandparents," Ms. Núñez nodded sympathetically. "But my mother always had plenty of stories about them, so it's not like I never got to know about them. Oh, look!" she pointed towards one of the shops on the left. "Señor Lujoso's is open! We should take a field trip for class one day."

Mr. Lains' house

Mr. Lains' house rested in the middle of the pine tree forest at the edge of a large subdivision, hidden from anyone on the road.

Justin smiled as he climbed out of the car. The bulldog statue on the porch, the kitchen window where you could watch people come and go, and the smell of pine were all staples of the times he and Terrence had visited.

Martin Lains opened the door before Justin even stepped onto the porch.

Rose had once remarked that Mr. Lains' pudgy belly combined with the roundness of his cheeks gave his lanky frame a grandfatherly look (although Rose had been seven when she had said this so it came out much cruder), this combined with his bad posture due to his poor back made him seem older than he actually was. As Justin approached the door, he noticed the white beard of stubble that stood out on his grandfather's face and wondered if he would grow out his beard the way it had been when Justin was little.

"Hello!" Mr. Lains waved to Ms. Núñez as she pulled out of the driveway. "Come on in, Justin."

Justin sighed as he stepped through the door, welcomed by the familiar musty scent of the house.

"How's it going, Pop Pop?" Justin asked, setting his backpack down and falling onto the couch.

149

"Pretty good," Mr. Lains nodded, settling himself into his recliner. "I started taking a painting class at the community center," he pointed to a painting of a violet on the wall. "I did that one last week."

"Cool," Justin nodded.

"So what do you want to do today, Justin?"

"I dunno," Justin shrugged.

Mr. Lains nodded again.

"How's Capes?" the older man asked.

"Good," Justin said. "Also big…"

"It's no public school that's for sure," Mr. Lains nodded. "Have you made friends?"

"Yeah, a couple," Justin smiled. "One of my friends, Eliza, she's super cool. She can read minds and it's kinda freaky, but she's really nice about it and tries to not do it on purpose. My other friend, Simon, he's super smart, but he gets super embarrassed about it. Mr. Wane called on him to answer a difficult question yesterday and he answered it correctly. His ears turned red from embarrassment."

Mr. Lains smiled. "What are they doing today?"

"Simon's probably playing video games… I don't know what Eliza's doing…" Justin actually did know what Eliza was doing, she was faking a headache so she could try and investigate one of the doctors, Melissa.

"Maybe next month they'd like to escape Capes and come with us on a tour of the best ice cream places nearby," Mr. Lains suggested.

"Really?" Justin sat up. "I mean, they'd probably like to!"

Two hours (and six shows) later

"Thanks again for the ice cream," Justin said, placing his bowl in the dishwasher.

"Of course!" the older man nodded. "Just remember what I said."

"Don't tell my Godparents I had ice cream for lunch," Justin smiled. "I won't."

"Good," Mr. Lains chuckled. "Anywhere you want to go or shall we continue binging whatever comes on the T.V.?"

"I don't really know where there is to go."

Mr. Lains nodded.

"Want a tour?"

Three hours later

Justin and Mr. Lains toured all of downtown Arenthia. After peeking into Tony's Pizza Plaza and Señor Lujoso's, passing by a nursery called Plant Time, and browsing the shelves of Valleyway Candies, they drove into downtown Capsburg.

Unlike the quaint little shops of Arenthia, the stores of Capsburg were bustling with shoppers of every kind. The toy store was full of little kids wearing capes of every length and color, the grocery was full of families buying goods, and the streets were flooded with people in an array of both normal clothes and costumes like circus performers. Everything about the city was thriving with life.

"When I was your age," Mr. Lains huffed, trying to keep up with Justin as they rushed across the crosswalk. "There was a fountain in the middle of the square. They had to remove it due to the last drought and the kids that got caught stealing coins to use on the games in the arcade. Wet quarters in an electric machine caused some malfunctions so the owners complained to the city government."

"Did you used to take coins from the fountain?" Justin asked jokingly.

"Now Justin!" Mr. Lains gave a fake gasp. "Why on earth would you think a thing like that?"

Justin giggled.

After growing hungry they'd decided to eat a late lunch at Tom's Diner and by the time the check came, it was time for Mr. Lains to drive Justin back to Capes.

"Thanks, Pop Pop," Justin said as he rummaged through his bag for his student I.D. "I had a lot of fun."

"No problem," he beamed. "I'll see you next month when you bring your friends."

"I'll see you next month," Justin promised as the gates opened.

Rec room: back building

"Justin!" Eliza waved him over to the couch she sat on with Annie.

"Hey," Justin smiled, settling onto the floor in front of her.

"How's your Grandpa?" Eliza asked.

"Pretty good," Justin said as Annie picked up her book and began to read. "He took me around Capsburg and Arenthia and showed me all the places you can get ice cream. He promised to eventually take me to each one."

"Cool!" Eliza's eyes glittered.

"He said I could bring a couple friends next time," Justin continued. "So you and Simon are invited to come with me."

"Would we get free ice cream?" Eliza smiled, her eyes sparkling.

"Definitely," Justin promised.

"I'm in," the glint in her eye shone brighter.

"Awesome!" Justin tried to ignore the bubbling excitement in his stomach. "Do you know where Simon is?"

"Gaming nook," she pointed to the alcove along the right wall. "One of the second years challenged him to a game."

"I'll ask him later," Justin nodded, glancing at Annie, who was still absorbed in her book. "How was… your homework?"

"Checking on Melissa," he thought.

"It took forever," Eliza groaned. "And I'm pretty sure I got half the answers wrong."

Based on the look she gave him Justin guessed that she hadn't gotten any information from Melissa.

Justin nodded disheartedly.

"It's fine," Eliza shrugged, her jaw tight. "I'll just have to work harder to get the right answers."

Chapter Seventeen
When one door closes…

"How many of you tried to be observant this week?" Mr. Johnson asked as everyone got seated.

A few kids raised their hands.

"Good," Mr. Johnson smiled. "Let's see what you remember."

He lifted a cardboard box off the ground and placed it on his desk.

"Who was wearing this?" he asked, pulling a bright blue wrist watch out of the box.

Bailey was the first to raise her hand.

"Yes, Bailey," Mr. Johnson gave her a nod.

"Miss Brush was wearing that."

"Yes!" Mr. Johnson smiled, causing Bailey to beam with pride. "Do you remember when?"

"Thursday?" she guessed.

"Right again!" Mr. Johnson smiled encouragingly. "Do you remember the color of her shoes?"

Bailey shook her head, clearly disappointed to have forgotten.

"They were brown," said a second-year.

"Correct," Mr. Johnson gave her a nod. "Good job, Mary. Does anyone remember what she was wearing in her hair?"

"A small barrette and three bobby pins," said a third-year boy.

"One small barrette and three bobby pins exactly. Good job Jeffery," Mr. Johnson smiled again. "Now, does anyone care to explain to the first years why we do this experiment?"

The girl next to Eliza raised her hand.

"Go ahead, Caitlyn," Mr. Johnson encouraged.

"Those who want to go into hero work need to be observant enough to be able to track down a villain," Caitlyn explained. "It's also helpful to those who want to be police or private eyes."

"Precisely," Mr. Johnson smiled. "Even in normal lives, being observant can help you get a better job."

Justin nodded, vaguely aware of the foreboding chill that had entered the room.

"Now," Mr. Johnson placed the watch on his desk. "Who was wearing this…"

That night: the library

"Do you think we should try and write down the prophecy?" Simon asked.

Justin sat up from where he had been laying on the floor.

"Why hadn't we thought of this sooner?" he marveled. "Our most valuable asset is handed to us on a silver platter and we forget about it!"

"It's too bad that we can't get the exact words," Eliza said, soberingly.

"Does nobody write prophecies down?" Justin asked.

"Unless they have paper when the prophecy's spoken, no," Eliza answered. "Either nobody remembers the exact words and the prophecy is forgotten or someone holds on to whatever shred of the prophecy they remember, but can't remember the full thing. Every once in a blue moon a prophecy will get re-spoken, but it's not common."

"You're still reading that book Mrs. Strong gave you," Simon deduced.

"Yeah," Eliza shrugged. "It helps me procrastinate doing homework."

"So how did the prophecy begin?" Justin asked.

157

"Well, Mrs. Strong came into the room," Simon recalled.

"And Mary Anne said her name, which got her attention," Eliza nodded.

"Then she started talking about how Blackglycerin wanted equality," Simon continued, writing it down as well as he could.

"'He wanted to change the world from the ground up,'" Justin quoted.

Eliza nodded.

"Then she said he had a lot of followers," she looked down at the table. "And that he… attacked a lot of people."

"Including my parents," Justin whispered.

"Yeah," Eliza muttered, refusing to look him in the eyes.

"Then she said that Blackglycerin was here at Capes," Simon said, breaking the silence. "And that someone in the room would be the one to stop him."

Justin nodded as he watched Simon finish writing.

"So all we have is exposition and a vague promise," Said Eliza flatly.

"At least we have *something*," Justin rationalized.

"There's nothing that will help us find him," Eliza argued. "Which means we have nothing to go on except our own research."

"We could try looking up articles from Blackglycerin's reign of terror," Simon suggested. "We can use the library computer."

"Why not just use our phones?" Justin asked.

"A school computer is given direct access to the internet and can't be traced back to us," Simon said, rising from the table.

"Fair enough," Eliza said, following him to the computer by the door.

Simon sat down and started typing.

"How do you know how to spell Blackglycerin?" Eliza asked.

"Well, black is B-L-A-C-K," Simon explained.

"Duh."

"And glycerin is a part of the word nitroglycerin, a compound of making bombs."

"So…" Eliza frowned.

"*So* I had looked up bomb ingredients, nothing suspicious about that," Simon laughed. "I found nitroglycerin and memorized the spelling. G-L-Y-C-E-R-I-N."

Eliza's eyes widened in surprise.

"Wow," she nodded, impressed. "You're a lot more serious about this than I thought you were."

"If someone's hiding from something bad they did, they should be brought to justice," Simon said seriously.

"I agree," Justin nodded. "People shouldn't be able to get away with crimes."

"I obviously agree too," she rolled her eyes, but Justin saw a smile tug on her lips. "I was just surprised how much thought Simon had put into this."

Simon looked over his shoulder and gave her a wide grin.

"Thanks," he turned back to the computer and hit search.

Two hundred and thirteen results.

Simon started scrolling through the recommended articles.

"That one," Justin pointed to a headline.

"'Local Reporter Spots Mastermind Behind Recent Attacks,'" Eliza read as Simon clicked on the link. "When is this from?"

"Nine years ago," Justin read the date under the heading.

"'After the recent attacks all over the world, people have begun looking for the leader of the group. Margaret Marry believes she spotted him.'" Simon read. "'During the attack on the Markston city hall, local reporter, Margaret Marry, was able to identify the leader of the group of terrorists. Though the man has yet to be identified, he has been nicknamed "Blackglycerin." After talking to Miss Marry, we were able to find out the meaning behind the nickname. "He was watching as the first bomb went off." Miss Marry stated. "He didn't even flinch as the explosion took over the building. Then someone else came up to him and whispered something to him. He nodded and the second guy pulled out a gun and fired, that's what set off the second bomb. At that point." Miss Marry continued. "I was hiding under the picnic table I had been eating at, but I noticed as he turned around that his face was riddled with scars. The funny thing was, he had covered some of the scars in a black paste that looked like gunpowder."

"'The group of terrorists was somehow able to plant explosions in and around the Markston city hall. Luckily no one was killed, though fifteen people were injured.'"

"Let's find a different article," suggested Justin.

Simon nodded and returned to the results page.

"Here's another one where they spotted him," he clicked on the link.

"'The most recent attack in the U.S, an attack on the San Antonio capitol building, led for a further investigation to try and catch the nefarious leader of the terrorists.'" Eliza read. "'A Texan detective decided to pull footage from a security camera across the street from the incident. The public statement included a picture from the pulled footage, shown below, of the man known as Blackglycerin.'"

"Here's the photo," Simon clicked on the expand button.

A grainy picture of a burning building filled the screen. In the middle of the street stood a man in a black trench coat.

"Can you zoom in?" Justin asked, leaning forward.

Simon clicked twice and the picture expanded. Even through the bad quality of the photo, it was apparent that something was off about his face. The shadows on his face were too dark, the lines too light, everything made him look unreal.

"How could he be here without anyone knowing?" Justin wondered out loud.

"I don't know," Simon frowned.

"I asked Mr. Fields if he thought someone was poisoning the food," Eliza said after a second of silence. "He said it could be a possibility."

Simon turned around, his eyes wide with alarm.

"Really?" he asked.

"Yeah," she nodded seriously. "He said it passively, but I think he meant it."

Justin frowned. The staff must be overconfident in their ability to find the villian if they're telling students they *might be getting poisoned.*

"It shouldn't be anything to worry about," Justin finally said, unsure whether he was trying to convince them or himself.

"Right," Eliza nodded.

An hour later

Justin and Eliza were the only ones left in the library. Simon had left to put the books he'd checked out in the dorm before dinner and the fifth year who'd been scanning the shelves had run out of the room after getting a phone call.

"Do you really think it's nothing to worry about?" asked Eliza as she picked up her bag.

Justin didn't answer for a second. Eliza glanced up from fiddling with the strap on her bag, her eyes wide.

"She's genuinely scared," Justin realized. The fact that Eliza, someone who never let things get to her, was letting him see how frightened she was scared Justin more than Mr. Fields' admission.

"We haven't seen any sign that there is," he shrugged. "So there's no reason to believe that we should be worried."

Eliza nodded unassuredly as they made their way downstairs.

"I hope you're right..." she fretted.

"Me too," Justin thought.

They opened the door to the cafeteria and collided with two people exiting.

"Oh no," Eliza whispered, stepping away from the girl she'd walked into.

Justin glanced to his left. Eliza seemed to be carved from stone as she stared at the floor. He looked back to the two girls they'd run into.

They were at least four years older than them, based on height alone (though Justin was short so who knows how accurate that is). The taller of the two girls gave them a perplexed look, as she tugged on a strand of her red hair. The second girl barely gave them a once-over, as if she were checking her dark makeup in a window, before smirking.

"Oh. Hello, Eliza," the second girl said coolly.

"Hi, Marian," Eliza mumbled.

"I see you've made a friend," she didn't look at him.

"Hi," Justin said awkwardly. "I'm Justin."

Marian glanced at him.

"Hi, Justin," the redhead said. "...I'm Amy."

Justin awkwardly returned her wave.

"You still have that childish streak in your hair," Marian ignored them, eyeing Eliza's hair with an amused look. "I'd have thought Mom and Dad would've made you take it out by now. Or have they even noticed it?"

The streak disappeared.

"Thought so," Marian smirked again as she walked away. Amy mouthed "sorry" and followed.

Eliza looked down at her shoes.

"I don't think she meant to be mean," Justin told her half-heartedly.

"She did," she looked up. "I heard her thoughts."

"Oh," Justin couldn't think of anything else to say.

"Yeah. That's my sister," she combed her fingers through her hair as the icy blue streak reappeared. "Miss entitled."

"Well don't listen to her," Justin shrugged. "She obviously doesn't know you."

She gave another shrug.

"Looks like we're having spaghetti," she motioned towards the chalkboard menu.

"We should grab a table," Justin nodded, accepting the change of conversation.

Eliza nodded and followed him to a table, resting her head in her hands as she sat.

"They better have garlic bread," Eliza grumbled.

Justin smiled.

Chapter Eighteen

… Another Door Opens

October: Wednesday

It was Sandwich Wednesday in the cafeteria. Twenty-two different kinds of sandwiches were being offered. The cafeteria was filled with chatter (mostly of "why isn't it Sandwich Saturday?").

"What sandwich would you like, hon?" asked the lady behind the counter.

"What sandwiches do you have with peanut butter?" Justin asked.

"Peanut butter, p b and j, fluffernutter, that's peanut butter and marshmallow fluff; peanut butter and honey, and the Elvis," she smiled at his perplexed face. "It's peanut butter and banana slices."

"I will have that. Thank you…" he glanced at the name tag. "Marta."

She smiled again and started making his sandwich.

"Marta…" Justin had an idea. "Have they been testing the food for poison?"

She looked up from her sandwich making, obviously startled by his question. She smoothed the features on her face and smiled simply.

"Yes, they have," she told him reassuringly. "Don't worry, you'll be fine... There's no real proof that kids are being poisoned, we're just checking to keep the parents from being worried."

Justin gave her a small smile.

"Here's your sandwich, hon," she passed him a sandwich on a plate. "Chips and drinks are on the snack bar."

"Thank you," he grabbed the plate and forced a smile.

"Marta said they're testing the food for poison," he whispered to Eliza as he sat down.

She nodded discreetly and continued talking to Bailey.

It only took nine minutes for Luke to start ranting about... something. Justin was deep in a trance of pretending to listen when something in the corner of his eye caught his attention.

A group of fifth-years was leaving the dining hall. At first glance it looked like they were walking arm in arm, you know as all pals do, but Justin, noticing the way two of the guys' heads drooped, deduced that they were being held up by the other three as if they couldn't walk on their own.

Justin glanced across the table at Simon, who glanced at the leaving boys and ever so discreetly inclined his head toward Eliza. Justin, without taking his eyes off of the retreating students, nudged her with his elbow. He saw her turn to face him in the corner of his eye and nodded in the boys' direction.

She gave a puzzled look but nodded. Justin turned back to Simon, who gave him a slow nod.

Two more people had been poisoned.

Two weeks later

Afternoons in the library were starting to become Justin's favorites. This afternoon in particular Justin and Simon were working on their History essays (Justin hadn't finished it and Simon was trying to perfect his) while Eliza (who had done hers in Study Hall, declared it perfect, and refused to look it over) was reading the book Mrs. Strong had lent her.

"I'm going to go browse the books," Justin said, abandoning his homework.

"There's a good selection of fiction in the back left corner," said Simon, not looking up from his paper.

"Or I can let you borrow my book on future seeing," Eliza offered, holding up the book lazily.

"Hard pass," Justin laughed.

He heard the book thump on the table as he made his way to the back wall and laughed again, quietly this time. He reached out and let his hand glide over the edge of the shelves. Something about the smooth wood under his fingers felt calming to Justin. He smiled to himself as he rounded the corner, scanning the shelves for fiction books. They had a series that he had read with the twins a couple of years ago on one of the shelves in the corner. He knelt, letting his fingers rest on the shelf as he read the titles.

"I know I've read these," he muttered, running his fingers across the shelf. "But I can't remember if I've read these?"

Sudden friction caused Justin to frown.

Justin leaned forward and studied the shelf. It didn't seem to have any flaws in the wood and Justin didn't have a splinter or anything, yet he was positive that he'd felt friction.

Cautiously, he ran his hand over the section again.

Friction.

Justin examined the area with his index finger.

"Eliza!" he called. "Simon! Come check this out!"

170

There was the sound of chairs moving against the carpet, an indication that they were getting up from the table and coming his way.

"Note to self:" Justin thought. *"My observation skills have improved."*

"What is it?" Simon appeared from behind the shelves.

"Come feel this," he waved them over. "There's bumps on this shelf."

"Bumps?" Eliza asked, touching the spot where he pointed. "Huh. Simon, feel this."

Justin moved to the side so Simon could reach.

"Interesting," Simon nodded, tracing the outline of the bumps with his finger.

"What?" Justin and Eliza asked harmoniously.

"The bumps form an arrow, look." Justin and Eliza leaned forward and watched as Simon used two fingers to trace a definite outline of an arrow.

"I wonder if it's a secret passage," Simon said, tapping his finger on the shelf. "The arrow could be pointing to the book you need to pull on to open it."

Eliza reached forward and pulled half of the books off the shelf.

"Nope," she shoved the books back into place.

Simon frowned and examined the shelf.

"Maybe you open it by pushing down on a secret panel," he suggested.

Justin reached past Eliza and pressed down on the shelf next to the arrow.

"Nothing," he sighed.

"You didn't do it hard enough," Eliza said, pushing his arm out of the way.

She positioned her arm over the shelf and pressed down using all of her weight. Then, the panel sank into the shelf with a small click. The three exchanged a surprised glance as the bottom half of the bookshelf sank into the floor.

"Well…" Justin said after a moment of shock. "Ladies first?"

"You know modern feminism says you should go first," Eliza frowned. "Otherwise, you insult the woman by implying she's weak."

"Oh. I-"

"I'm kidding," she smiled at him. "I can go first if you two are too chicken."

Before either boy could defend themselves, she disappeared into the passageway.

"That was serendipitous," Simon blinked.

"What does that word even mean?" Justin frowned.

"It means a lot of things," Simon shrugged and crawled in after Eliza.

"Well okay then," Justin chuckled, crouching down as he entered the passage behind them.

"About time," Eliza said as they stood. "Look, there's a passageway there and a lever here," she pointed to the silver lever on the wall. "I'm guessing it closes the passage from the inside."

Justin scanned the small room as he finished brushing the lint off his pants. It was big enough for maybe ten people to stand comfortably in, with white walls and LED lights overhead. The hall next to the passage they'd come through stretched past Justin's view.

"Shall we explore?" Simon asked, a mischievous glint in his eyes.

"I thought you'd never ask!" Eliza smiled. She pulled the lever downwards, sealing them in, before heading down the hall.

"This hall runs the entire length of the library," Simon said, running his hand along the wall as they walked single file down the passage.

"The real question is, where does it lead?" Justin asked.

Eliza stopped suddenly. "There's a room here."

The room at the end of that hall was the same as the last one, but smaller. The only real difference was there wasn't a lever on the wall.

"Weird," Justin muttered.

Justin crossed his fingers, hoping they'd ask him what was weird because he'd come to a smart conclusion.

"What?" Simon asked to Justin's delight.

"If this is a secret room…" he motioned to the room. "Is this the only one? And if not, is it connected to the others?"

Simon surveyed the room with a wide-eyed stare.

"What if…" he pondered aloud. "It's another hidden button."

"Could be…" Eliza nodded, running a hand over the wall beside her.

Justin eyed the wall beside him as Eliza found the panel.

"Here," Eliza pressed the panel into the wall.

A secret panel opened beside the panel to reveal a lever.

"Huh," Justin stared at the lever in shock. "It's a lever."

"How observant," Eliza said dryly. "Shall we try it?"

She reached forward and pulled the lever upwards.

"Nothing happened," Justin frowned, feeling anticlimactic.

"Turn around," Simon laughed.

Justin spun around and gaped at the open trapdoor on the floor, with several footholds appearing in the wall, leading down the trapdoor.

"Oh," Justin giggled.

"I guess that's why they didn't put it closer to the lever," Eliza said, eyeing the hole.

"It *is* slightly dangerous," Simon agreed. "Should we explore it?"

"Hang on," Justin frowned as a realization hit him. "The prophecy said Blackglycerin was *hiding* at Capes. What if he's hiding in one of the passages?"

Simon and Eliza both fell silent.

"Well..." Simon chewed his bottom lip. "What do we do?"

"Search the tunnels?" Eliza suggested.

175

"Is that safe?" Simon worried. "If he is in the passages."

"I could protect us," Justin said after a minute. Something inside him told him that he would be able to keep them safe, though whether that something was foolishness or actual insight was anyone's guess. "I can make a force field to shield us from any unseen attacks."

Eliza nodded, rolling her shoulders.

"He's right," she nodded. "If needed, I can use telekinesis to stall him."

"So when do we search the passages?" Simon asked.

"How about Saturday?" Justin offered. "There are no classes then and the older students all head to town for the day."

"They'll be less likely to notice us gone," Simon nodded in agreement.

"Okay, Saturday," Eliza said decisively. She pulled the lever back up and watched as the handholds in the wall filled back in and the hole in the floor sealed itself.

"Okay," Simon nodded, seeming unsurprised as they reentered the first room. "So the lever always disappears."

Simon located the panel on the wall, revealed the lever, and reopened the passage.

"Oh, boo," Eliza joked as they got back to the table. "No one stole my book."

"Throw it in the passages and hope it disappears," Justin joked.

"That would scare me more than having to read it," Eliza shuddered.

Chapter Nineteen
Behind the Walls

Boy's rec room: 9 p.m

"Do you have a flashlight I could borrow?" Justin asked Kyle as Friday night rolled around.

"Yeah, why?" Kyle asked, turning to face him.

"Eliza challenged me to a flashlight duel," Justin lied.

"What's a flashlight duel?" Kyle asked, suddenly looking very intrigued.

"I don't know," Justin shrugged. "But if you find out, let me know, I'm hoping to win."

Noon: the next day

Justin waited by the kitchen doors for Marta. Turns out, if you know the right person, you can get the good snacks, the kind of snacks meant for teachers. Because the teachers didn't eat many snacks, some of the kitchen staff were willing to sneak the disregarded treats to the kids. The only person who didn't want the students to have the snacks was the head chef, Stephen, since it was his job to make sure the students didn't get to them, but he was nice enough to pretend to not know the kitchen staff had been raiding the cupboard.

"Here ya go, hon," Marta said as she emerged from behind the kitchen doors. "I've got chips, waters, and a couple candy bars."

"Thanks, Marta!" Justin said, shoving the snacks into his bag.

"No problem," she gave him a wink. "Have fun on your picnic."

Library: one p.m

"You got the stuff?" Simon asked as Justin entered the library.

"Yeah," Justin held up his bag. "Do you have the other stuff?"

"Yes, now can we please stop talking like this?" Eliza faked a groan.

"Sure," "Okay," The boys laughed.

"Great," she sighed. "Let's get going."

Eliza led the way to the back of the library, settled onto the floor in front of the shelves, and put her hand over the panel. She paused before pressing the panel into the shelf.

"Ready?" she asked.

"Yep," Justin gave her a nod, as he formed a small force field over his hands.

"Okay," she took a deep breath and opened the passageway. Justin gawked at the shelves one more time as his friends entered the passages. The entrance was low enough to not be seen if you were behind any of the other bookshelves and the mechanisms in them were quiet enough that they didn't draw any attention from anyone else in the room.

"Do you think we should check this room for another passage?" Simon asked as they stood.

"Why?" Justin asked.

"I don't think the passages would be in one straight path," Simon explained. "It's more likely to be a series of interconnected rooms with entrances and exits in different places."

"What makes you think that?" Eliza asked.

"If all the hidden rooms were in the same place on each floor, someone would notice a pattern in the amount of space unaccounted for," Simon shrugged. "It makes more sense to have the rooms more spread out, with one room having multiple entrances and exits to passageways, that way, it's less likely that all the rooms would be discovered."

He pulled a notebook out of his backpack.

"What's that for?" Justin asked as Simon opened to the first page.

"Making a rough draft of a map of Capes," he turned the pages towards them so they could see the pencil sketches he'd made. "I want to try and sketch where each hidden room is."

"Smart," Eliza gave him a smile.

Simon blushed slightly and mumbled thanks.

"Okay, so we search this room first?" Eliza asked.

"I'll take the wall with the hallway," Justin offered.

"I'll search the back wall," Eliza said.

"I-" Simon stopped. "Okay."

The hardest part about searching for an invisible panel was (aside from the invisible part) the fact that you couldn't feel the panel itself, only the braille-like indicators that told you the panel was there.

"Aha!" cried Eliza after three minutes of searching.

The panel was by the corner between the back wall and the hallway and sank into the wall with a soft click, like pushing the shutter button on a camera, as a lever popped out of its hiding spot.

"Simon, you can do the honors," Eliza suggested. "Justin, you're on defense."

"Right," he focused on the area around them and formed a shield. It was pale blue and had a couple of holes, but Justin strained his focus and fixed them.

"Cool," Eliza nodded, studying the shield. "I'm on offense."

Simon pulled the lever and a small, square opening appeared above them.

"Eliza, how about you go first," Justin extended his shield to allow them to enter the room above. "Then Simon. I'll try and cover you from down here."

Eliza gave a quick nod, tried her grip on the footholds, and scaled the wall. Justin made sure the shield covered her as Simon tucked his notebook into his bag and followed her, slowly as if he were afraid to fall.

Justin took another deep breath, continuing to concentrate on the force field, and carefully made his way upstairs, weakening the area of the shield around him to better protect the room above.

The first thing Justin noticed when he emerged from the trapdoor was how small of a space his shield encapsulated them in.

"Sorry," he muttered, extending his shield to cover the length of the room.

"Shhh," Eliza whispered, her ear pressed against the wall.

"We're behind the gaming nook," Simon explained. "We're trying to figure out if they can hear us."

"Ah," Justin said in a hushed tone.

"I don't hear anything," Eliza whispered.

"They might be in between rounds," Simon explained.

"Rounds?" Eliza frowned.

"Of the game."

"Oh." There were muffled yells from the other side of the wall.

"So if we yell, they can hear us," Justin perceived.

"So we can't get mad at each other while in the tunnels," Eliza smirked playfully.

"We can't be irrationally loud," Simon corrected.

"Tomato, potato," she shrugged. "Mad people *are* irrational people."

"Do you think that this is the only room on this floor?" Justin asked, noticing that there was no visible hallway on this floor.

"There might be another one," Simon frowned. "But the entrance might not be on this floor."

"Okay," Eliza agreed. "So, how about we check this room for levers and move on." She turned and started examining the walls. The boys quickly followed her example.

"Here!" Justin called as soon as he met friction beneath his fingers.

There was another trap door above their heads.

Eliza made her way upstairs first.

"Woah," her voice came from above them.

"What?" Simon quietly called upstairs.

"It's really big up here," she said, poking her head through the trapdoor. "Come see."

"Woah," Justin gaped as he entered the room.

"It's got to be the length of the entire floor," Simon said giddily.

"Except for the stairwell," Justin scrunched up his eyebrows, trying to compare sizes in his head.

Eliza held a hand up for them to be quiet and put her ear to the wall.

"I think they're watching a movie," she announced. "I can hear noise from the projector."

"Should we check for other exits?" Justin asked. "Just in case?"

"Probably," Eliza shrugged.

After ten minutes of searching, they finally found an exit that led out by the stairwell, with a door that slowly merged with the wall, gaining no attention from any possible person in the stairwell. They sealed both entrances giving themselves a couple seconds headstart in case someone tried to enter the room and took a break to let Justin rest from forming the force field.

"You okay, Justin?" Eliza asked.

Justin nodded wearily and slouched to the floor. He could feel beads of sweat forming on his forehead, but he hadn't started glitching yet, so he deemed himself fine.

"Anybody want snacks?"

Ten minutes later

"We should keep searching," Eliza eventually said, shoving her empty chip bag into her pocket and rising to her feet.

"Yeah," Justin nodded, feeling shaky but determined.

"Are you sure you're okay?" Eliza asked, helping him stand up as Simon relocated the lever.

"I'm fine, just a little drained."

"Okay…" Eliza frowned.

The three made their way back downstairs, Eliza in the lead, opening the trapdoors, and Simon taking up the rear, adding to his sketches whenever he could. After making their way past the library and down to the front floor, they stared in shock at…

"A tunnel?" Eliza said, staring at the opening in the ground perplexed.

"Should we see where it goes?" Justin asked, peering down the dark pathway in front of them.

"Well, we have flashlights…" Simon shrugged.

"Right," Eliza pulled her flashlight out of her pocket.

The tunnel lit up from the single beam of light. Eliza pointed the beam towards the ceiling as they descended into the ground.

"Huh. No overhead lights," Eliza remarked.

Justin nodded, trying to steady his breathing as the darkness sealed them in.

"It's not really a tunnel," Justin told himself. *"It's more of a long room."*

In fact, the walls were the same color as the other passages and the floor had the same tile pattern. The only real difference was the lack of light.

Justin and Simon followed Eliza through the tunnel, which eventually slanted upwards until they emerged in another secret room.

"Do you think we're in the main building?" Eliza asked as Justin sealed off the tunnel with his shield.

"Probably," Simon crouched down and started sketching a map of the school grounds. "Though the hard part will be figuring out where in the building we are."

Chapter Twenty
After Further Investigation...

Turns out, the secret room was behind 102, 104, and 108, and part of the girl's bathroom.

"I wondered why there was this weird wall there," Eliza nodded, closing the entrance to the bathroom.

Justin discovered the second lever around the middle of the room.

"Another tunnel," he said, staring at the stairs that descended into the floor.

"Guys," Simon said, drawing their attention to a third lever. A tug on the lever at the other end of the hall revealed a trap door leading upwards.

"Tunnel or ladder first?" Eliza asked.

"Let's search upstairs first," Justin said. "That way we don't have to come back if we find another exit."

Thirty minutes later

The second and third floors had long, jagged halls that covered the length of the front part of the building with a small room on each end. They both had entrances in supply closets. The fourth floor had one small room with another entrance in a supply closet.

Despite searching the whole building, they hadn't seen any evidence that someone else had been in the tunnels. In fact, the passages were so dusty they looked as if they hadn't been used in decades.

After taking another break, Justin followed Eliza and Simon back into the ground and blinked in surprise when he saw three more tunnels.

"Okay, so that one must lead to the girls' dorms," Eliza said, pointing to the tunnel to her right. "And that one to the boys' dorm," she pointed to the left tunnel. "The question is where does that one lead?"

"Probably somewhere off campus," Simon shrugged.

"Let's explore that one first then," Justin said, switching on his flashlight. "If Blackglycerin *is* hiding here, wouldn't he want to be closer to the exit?"

"I would," Eliza nodded.

Justin tried to strengthen his shield but was only able to fill a couple of the holes. He bit his lip but didn't say anything. The shield, like Justin, was growing weaker.

End of the tunnel

"I don't see anything up ahead," Simon said from upfront. "I think it's a dead end."

As they came upon the end of the passageway, they were met by two more tunnels, one on each side stretching at an angle back towards where they came from. Eliza stepped in front of Simon and started searching the walls.

"Do you think there's an exit here?" Justin asked as she continued to feel the wall.

"I *know* there's an exit here," she pushed the secret panel into the wall.

"We didn't walk that far," Simon frowned. "I don't think we're off-campus."

Eliza shrugged, hand on the lever.

"Shall I?" she asked, giving them a mischievous smile.

"Wait!" Justin said, blocking the lever with his hand. "We need a plan."

"We have a plan," she shrugged. "Explore."

"What if the exit lets out into broad daylight?" Justin said, swatting her hand away from the lever. "We could be spotted."

"You're right," Simon nodded, contemplating their next move. "I'll go. That way only one of us gets caught. I'll go up, figure out where we are, and come right back."

"What if you're spotted?" Eliza fretted.

190

"Then I leave the tunnel," Simon stood straighter. "Just make sure you seal the tunnel after me so no one else finds it and continue searching the tunnels."

Justin wanted to argue but decided against it when he saw the determined glare Simon had put on. He tried to replace the frown on his face with an encouraging smile but was certain it looked more like a grimace.

"Good luck," he said as Eliza pulled the lever.

Simon handed Justin his notebook.

"I'll be right back," he promised, climbing towards the open sky that rose beyond the open trapdoor.

Justin peered so far upwards he could feel his neck beginning to stiffen. Simon reached the top and cautiously poked his head out of the tunnel. Justin glanced at Eliza, who had her hand poised over the lever, ready to make sure their exit strategy was in play.

Simon froze at the top, then began to climb back down the ladder.

"We're under the fountain," he said as Eliza closed the exit. "The one on the right-hand side when you exit. The trapdoor is to the left of the fountain, it's an exit that gets you outside of the security systems. Except for the main gate."

"The gate locks at eleven, right?" Justin asked.

"And reopens at six," Simon nodded.

"So… it's an escape route you can only use during certain times?" Eliza cocked her head to the side. "That seems kinda useless."

"You never know, it could come in handy," Justin shrugged.

"So…. left or right?" Simon asked, motioning to the two tunnels adjacent to them.

Eliza shrugged as Justin handed the notebook back to Simon.

"Right?" Justin offered.

"Sounds good," Eliza agreed, making her way down the tunnel.

A little while later

After taking the long trek down the tunnel leading to the boys' dorms, they took another break to let Justin rest. Justin sank to the ground as Eliza and Simon kept their eyes on the exits which they'd left unopened. Eliza crouched next to Justin and started refiling through his backpack.

"Here," she said, dropping a bag of chips in his lap. "You need to eat, you're shaking."

Justin nodded, noticing the tremor in his hands for the first time as he picked up the bag.

192

"Simon," he opened the bag. "How many more tunnels do you think there are?"

"Two that we know of," Simon studied his map. "There should be one that takes us from the room in the main building to the boys' dorm and the one that leads from the girls' dorm to the fountain."

"Okay," Justin sighed.

"Are you going to be okay?" Eliza asked.

"Yeah," He nodded. "I just might need to spend some time in the glitch room."

"Maybe we should explore them later..." Simon fretted.

"No," Justin waved his concerns away. "I'll be fine."

"Okay…" Eliza stood, still frowning. "Let's be quick though."

As they headed off and explored the tunnel leading to the girls' dorm, Justin started to feel his legs go numb. By the time they emerged in the secret room next to the girls' dorm, he was leaning heavily on Eliza.

"Thanks," he muttered, leaning against one of the walls.

"No problem," she tried to not look concerned, but Justin saw her eyes flicker towards him. "You okay for searching the other tunnel?"

"Yeah, yeah," he nodded. "I'll be fine."

And then he passed out.

Nurses' ward

Justin blinked as white light flooded his vision.

"Good, you're awake."

Justin turned towards the voice and saw Martin, the nurse, standing nearby.

"How long was I out?" Justin asked, sitting up.

"About thirty minutes since your friends brought you in," he reached forward and felt the pulse in Justin's wrist. "Your heart rate has slowed down a bit from when I last checked it, that's a good sign. Can you tell me what happened?"

"We... Eliza, Simon, and I were practicing for a flashlight duel..." Justin fibbed. "And I thought I could try and use a force field to help me win... I guess I over-extended myself."

Martin nodded.

"Did the shield help protect you from the light at all?" he asked.

"Not really, but I kept hoping it would."

"That's probably how you over-extended yourself," Martin picked a water bottle off of the table next to the cot. "Drink plenty of water and get some sleep, you'll be fine as long as you don't continue to overexert yourself."

Justin took the water and stood. "Thank you."

"Sure thing," the nurse nodded.

Justin headed to leave but paused. There was a girl, a second-year by Justin's guess, passed out on a cot. Her skin was tinted green, as if he was suffering from seasickness.

He heard footsteps coming his way and walked off towards the stairwell, where found Eliza waiting for him.

"You okay?" she asked as she followed him downstairs.

"I think so," he shrugged. "Can't tell yet. I told him I used the shield for a flashlight duel."

"Smart," Eliza nodded. "Simon found a clue."

"What kind of clue?"

"Well, we were exploring the last tunnel after we brought you to the hospital ward," Eliza explained. "And Simon noticed the floor in the tunnel wasn't as dusty, so we went back one passage and found a dusty footprint that wasn't ours."

"How do you know it wasn't ours?"

"It was an adult-sized shoe print," Eliza said.

"So someone's using the tunnels to poison kids…" Justin froze. "What do we do to stop him?"

"We can't tell anyone until we have sustainable proof," Eliza shrugged. "Otherwise we lose credibility."

"So… What?" Justin asked.

"So we keep working to find proof."

Chapter Twenty-One
A Day with Papa Strikes

"Justin and Simon?" a teacher asked as the two exited the main building.

"Yeah," They answered.

"I'm Mr. Fields, I'll be your ride to Mr. Lain's house today," he gave them a brilliant smile, displaying cream-colored teeth. "I have Eliza in my class, so I know her already..."

He faltered for a second, his eyes frowning as he continued to smile.

"Where is Miss Thistle?" he asked.

Justin felt Simon give him a worried glance.

"She had to use the bathroom," Justin said after a beat.

Eliza was actually in the girls' dorm grabbing a notebook. She was using the secret passages to get from there to the main building, because in her words "living dangerously made her feel alive."

"Ah," Mr. Fields nodded.

Just then Eliza burst out of the building, leaving the doors rattling in her wake.

"Sorry I'm late!" she gasped.

"It's okay, better to go now instead of having to go in the car," Mr. Fields said, smiling, rummaging through his pockets for his keys.

Eliza's brows dipped into a slight frown.

"Bathroom," Justin mouthed.

She nodded.

"Okay!" Mr. Fields said, pulling his keys out of one of his pockets. "Car's out by the gate."

Mr. Lains' house

Martin Lains opened the door with a grin so wide Justin thought his face would split into pieces.

"Hello!" he sang. "You must be Simon."

He stuck out his hand for Simon to shake.

"I'm Mr. Lains, but you can call me Martin or Papa or Justin's grandpa," He chuckled lightly. "Justin told me that you're really smart," he released Simon's hand. "Do you play chess?"

"No sir," Simon said as they followed Mr. Lains into the house.

198

"Well then, I'll have to teach you," he turned to Eliza. "And you must be the powerful Eliza."

"I don't know about powerful," Eliza said humbly, but Justin noticed the twinkle in her eyes.

"I have a hunch that you're more powerful than you let on," Mr. Lains said heartily.

He turned to Justin.

"And I'm sorry young man, I don't seem to remember your name," he frowned.

"Hi, Pop Pop," Justin giggled.

"Hi, Justin," Mr. Lains smiled, wrapping Justin into a quick hug. "How are you?"

"Pretty good," Justin said as he sank onto the couch.

"Good," Mr. Lains smiled, settling himself into his chair. "So what have you three hooligans been up to outside of classes?"

Justin cast a questioning glance to Simon and Eliza.

"We're in an art club." Simon offered.

"We've been doing watercolors!" Eliza added.

"Ooh," Mr. Lains nodded thoughtfully. "I've always wanted to try watercolors."

"Don't," Simon grimaced. "It's really hard."

"It's only hard when you add too much water," Eliza said pointedly.

"Or if you're just bad at art," Justin joked.

"Sure," Simon laughed, giving Justin a cross-eyed look.

"So I was thinking," Mr. Lains said after the laughter died down. "I'd take you three to the park this afternoon. After getting ice cream, of course."

"Of course," Eliza repeated as Simon let out a whoop.

"Until then," Mr. Lains continued. "How about we play a round of dominoes?"

"Sure!" Justin said, jumping up to retrieve the box of dominoes from the hall closet.

"I haven't played with dominoes in years," he heard Eliza say as he pulled the box off its shelf.

"I've never played," Simon said as Justin reentered the room.

"It's pretty easy," Justin said, pulling the lid off the box and letting the pieces fall onto the coffee table with a pleasing plethora of clinking sounds.

Everyone settled around the table as Mr. Lains began to explain the rules of the game (with Justin chiming in with how they played at the Willows' house).

Justin, to his own surprise and delight, won the first game. Eliza, to no one's surprise, was somehow good at the game, despite it relying primarily on chance, and won the next four rounds.

"Gah!" Mr. Lains gave a fake, deep-throated groan. "Beaten again!"

"I don't understand how you keep winning!" Simon pouted. "Are you hiding a stash of dominoes under the table?"

"No," Eliza stood, showing the empty floor beneath her. "I'm just a natural-born winner."

"One more round?" Justin asked as Eliza plopped back down.

"I thought it was ice cream time," Simon suggested, eyes glittering hopefully.

"Isn't it too early for ice cream?" Eliza frowned.

"It's never too early for ice cream at my house," Mr. Lains said in a wise tone.

"So it's ice cream time?" Simon said, bouncing excitedly in his seat.

"It appears so!" Mr. Lains laughed. "I'll go grab my wallet and keys and take you hoodlums to Mr. Frozen's."

"Should we tell him?" Eliza asked in a hushed tone as Mr. Loans disappeared into his room. "About the prophecy?"

"I don't know..." Justin frowned. "We could."

"What if you did and he told someone?" a voice in his head said.

"What if he helps us find Blackglycerin?" he argued.

"You could get in trouble with the teachers!"

"We could end up in trouble without someone helping us!"

Eliza was watching him with a curious look on her face.

"It's not like the staff doesn't know about the prophecy," she rationalized. "We shouldn't get into trouble unless we tell him about the passages and the... you know."

The footprint they'd found. Justin nodded.

"She's right," Simon agreed. "It couldn't hurt to tell him."

"Okay then," Justin released a sigh of relief.

Picnic table in Langford Park

"Mr. Lains?" Eliza asked, pausing to stop a trail of ice cream from reaching her fingers. "Did you hear about the prophecy?"

"The one at Capes," Justin clarified

"No, I don't think I have," Mr. Lains lowered his hand that held his ice cream. "At least not in recent years. I doubt you're talking about the one from when I was in school."

"No, this prophecy is from our orientation day..." Simon said, awkwardly brushing some hair out of his face.

Mr. Lains' eyebrow twitched in surprise.

"Oh?" He questioned.

Justin looked down at his cup of ice cream, guilt flooding his chest.

"Crap," he thought. *"I should have told him last time I visited."*

"How do y'all know about this prophecy?" Mr. Lains asked.

"We were there when it was delivered," Eliza said, feigning nonchalance as she bit into her cone.

"It was after the ceremony of powers," Justin disclosed. "Mrs. Strong came in and looked... uh..."

"Misty-eyed," Simon finished.

"Misty-eyed," Justin amended. "Then she just delivered the prophecy."

"Aha..." Mr. Lains nodded, still frowning. "And what did this prophecy say?"

"It said that a villain is hiding at Capes," Justin leaned forward for dramatic effect. "And that one of us would stop him."

There were a couple seconds of silence, the only sound was of Simon slurping the remnants of his ice cream.

"So what are you three doing about it?" Mr. Lains eventually asked.

"Well…" Eliza stopped, giving Justin a hesitant glance. "We're trying to find him."

"Because!" Justin rushed to add. "No one on staff has bothered to."

"How do you know that?" Mr. Lains asked. "They wouldn't tell the students if they were doing an investigation."

"Mrs. Strong has a daughter, Amber," Eliza shrugged. "Kids don't keep secrets. And Mrs. Strong would've told Amber. Amber was the one who told us the prophecy was real."

Justin held his breath as Mr. Lains pondered his response, prepared for a rebuke.

"As proud as it makes me when I hear that y'all are doing what you think is honorable," Mr. Lains stirred his melted ice cream in its cup. "You three need to promise me that if you find trouble you'll run the other way and tell an adult."

"Of course!" Simon nodded seriously.

Eliza frowned but agreed.

Mr. Lains looked Justin in the eyes.

"Crap," Justin thought. *"If you can read my mind, I'm sorry. I'll try and stay out of trouble, I promise."*

"Justin?" Mr. Lains asked.

"Whew," Justin thought before replying, "I promise I'll try and stay out of trouble."

"Good," Mr. Lains turned to gaze at all three of them. "Just because you're children doesn't mean you're safe. It's good for you to learn that now rather than later."

Mr. Lains's hardened stare softened as he noticed the frightened look on Simon's face.

"Play it as safe as you can," Mr. Lains advised, adding a lighter tone to his voice. "Try and stay out of trouble and trouble won't come for you. And if there is trouble, tell an adult you can trust. Now, anything else you need to tell me about?"

Simon gave another frightened look to Justin and Eliza.

"Well, some people think someone's poisoning the food," Eliza said, chewing on her bottom lip.

"Why?" Mr. Lains seemed startled.

"A couple of students have passed out during meals," Simon explained. "One of the older students said he overheard someone saying they had been poisoned..."

"So there's no substantial evidence," Mr. Lains said, his eyes betraying his obvious relief. "It's just a rumor."

"But rumors can be based in fact," Justin countered, remembering Marta telling him that they'd been testing the food.

"And people will believe them even if they're not," Mr. Lains reasoned.

He let out a heavy sigh. "Don't worry about something that might be false until you have proof that it's real. You're kids, you shouldn't have to worry about things like this."

An hour later

"Do you think we shouldn't have told him?" Justin fretted. "About the rumors?"

"He won't tell anyone," Eliza said confidently.

"Yeah, he has no reason to tell anyone," Simon agreed.

"No, I mean I read his mind and he wasn't thinking about telling Mr. Whitaker or anything," Eliza explained. "We can trust him."

Justin smiled to himself.

"So it *was* a good idea," he said more to himself than to his friends.

"Getting ice cream was a good idea," Simon rubbed his stomach. "I think your grandpa might be my new favorite person."

Chapter Twenty-Two
Listening Through the Walls

"One more time!" Mr. Wire said.

Justin jumped up and down, letting his limbs fly willy nilly. First period wasn't even over yet and he and the entire class were exhausted. To Justin's left, Eliza was rubbing sleep from her eyes.

"Ready Miss Thistle?" Mr. Wire asked.

"Aye aye," Eliza smirked, giving a fake salute.

"Okay everyone line up," Justin gave Eliza a thumbs up as he stepped back into his spot in line. "And three... two... one... go!"

Justin decided at that moment that obstacle course day was his favorite. Obstacle course day came once a semester as a day that tried to challenge what students had learned in class so far. Other than being drenched in sweat before ten in the morning, it was perfect.

Eliza levitated a small, rainbow-colored ball into the air, all of her attention on Justin, who gave her a small, curt nod. Her questioning look turned into a smirk.

With the smallest flick of her wrist, Eliza sent the ball hurling towards Justin. As fast as he could, Justin clapped his hands together and pulled them apart as a portal expanded between them. The ball disappeared into his portal and the second it did Justin got rid of his first portal and made another over Clara.

Clara, somehow caught off guard, was almost hit in the head, but managed to open a portal and send the ball towards Zachariah, who sent it towards Kathryn. The ball made its way back and forth down the line before ending up in Flora's hands.

Eliza ran between the two lines and tagged Abigail, who repeated the course and tagged Luke.

After a couple people who only had telekinesis had run the course, it was Justin's turn.

He stretched out his hand, poised to run as Bailey ran towards him. She came to a stop beside him and high-fived his hand.

Justin tossed the ball in the air and sent it soaring towards Clara.

He watched, poised on the balls of his feet as the ball zapped from portal to portal. Justin started running the second the ball got to Patrick.

"Go Justin!" He heard Bailey cheer from behind him.

He was beaming when he reached the end of the row. Flora opened a portal above his head, letting the ball spiral towards him. Justin levitated the ball as he tagged Patrick, taking his spot in the line as he continued the course.

"Fourteen minutes!" Mr. Wire said as Holly finished the course. "Well done! That will be the time to beat for next semester's obstacle course. And! I'm pretty sure it's the best score a first-year class has gotten!"

As the class burst into applause, Justin turned to Eliza and gave her a thumbs-up before turning to find Simon. Instead of finding Simon, he made eye contact with Bailey, who blushed and gave him a small wave.

Justin blinked and waved back.

"Huh…" Justin thought as Simon walked towards him. *"That was…"*

"Okay!" Mr. Wire said, interrupting Justin's thought. "Off to your next class!"

"But the bell hasn't rung yet," Luke frowned.

"Yes, but you've got more obstacle courses to do," Mr. Wire said, corralling them out of the room. "And you might wanna see what's in store for you."

"He's up to something," Eliza whispered to Justin as they headed downstairs.

"How do you know?" Justin whispered back.

"I read it in his thoughts. He was trying to cover his thoughts… I think something bad happened."

Lunch

"You're wrong!" Annie said, shaking the table as she slammed her fists on its surface. "Captain Cosmo was *WAYYY* better when Caroline Winters had the title!"

"No, no, no!" Mary Anne said, shaking her head, sending her red curls flying. "Robert Calvin had more powers and he defeated the Vorpit King!"

"SO?" Annie yelled. "Caroline Winters had more control over her powers and defeated more villains! Plus! Robert Calvin only defeated the Vorpit King with the help of Scarlett Lynx!"

"Annie, you're yelling," Kyle said, rolling his eyes.

"So?" Annie said, turning to face her twin. "I-"

She was cut off by yells from the other side of the room. Justin was on his feet before the teachers made it to the victim.

"Everyone relax!" Mr. Wane yelled to the crowd. "She's just fainted."

Stephanie, who was taking her turn waiting in the cafeteria in case something like this happened, helped a third-year stand to her feet. Martin, dressed in bright blue scrubs, shined a light in the girl's eyes and said something inaudible to Stephanie. She had started to lead her out of the room when gasps sounded from behind Justin.

211

"We have another fainter!" called one of Terrence's friends, Peyton. He bent down and helped up a brunet boy.

Martin rushed over and helped Peyton carry him out of the building.

"Everyone stay where you are!" Louisa, the head of the kitchen staff, yelled. "Don't eat anything!"

Justin turned to Eliza and Simon.

"Oh no," Eliza muttered.

"Poison," Justin whispered.

Room 309: force fields

"Attention students," Mr. Whitaker's voice called out through the P.A system. "Despite the incidents that occurred during lunch today, there is no need to worry. The students who passed out had extreme allergic reactions and will be fine. Enjoy the rest of obstacle course day and remember: 'Vous Fabrique il ce loin.'"

"Whazzat mean?" Luke frowned.

"'You've made it this far,'" Mary Anne translated.

"Ominous," one of the girls frowned.

"Let's get started," Ms. Drills said, chewing her lip.

212

"Does she seem fidgety to you?" Bailey whispered from beside Justin.

"Yeah," Justin nodded. "A little bit."

"Weird," Bailey frowned as Ms. Drills began to explain how the course worked. "Mr. Wire was acting strange too."

"He was," Justin agreed, remembering what Eliza had told him about Mr. Wire trying to cover his thoughts.

"What's made everyone so jumpy?" Bailey wondered aloud.

"I wish I knew," Justin said mournfully.

"Okay!" Miss Drills gave them a painfully forced smile. "Any questions about the course?"

End of seventh period

Everyone anxiously broke out of room 309 as soon as the bell rang. The teacher's anxieties had begun to spread to the students, settling throughout the school like a fever of stress.

"Well, that was a fun course," Bailey said, feigning optimism.

"Yeah," Kyle agreed. "I just wish that there-"

213

He was cut off as someone bumped him on the stairwell.

"Sorry." The guy muttered, hurrying past them.

"You're good," Kyle said. "I wish Miss Drills hadn't made us make so many shields. I never want to make another shield."

"Fair enough," Bailey shrugged, as they entered the Spanish room.

"¡Hola classe!" Señorita Núñez smiled as they entered the room.

Justin frowned. Señorita Núñez was generally well put together, but today her hair was frizzy and she looked as if she hadn't slept last night. And despite the smile she gave them, Justin couldn't help but get the feeling she was just as on edge as the rest of the teachers were.

"What on earth is stressing them out?"

October 31st

"Ready?" Simon called through the bathroom door.

"Yep!" Justin said, adjusting his mask.

Simon flung open the door and let Justin step out.

214

"Ta-da!" Simon sang, arms held out to show off his superhero costume, complete with a mask, cape, and foam abs.

"Nice," Justin smiled, giving Simon a pair of thumbs-ups.

"But aren't we already superheroes?" Justin thought to himself.

"And you're a ninja!" Simon gave Justin's outfit an approving nod. "Awesome!"

"Thank you," Justin gave him a curt nod before launching into a series of kicks, jumps, and punches.

"Wonderful demonstration Justin," Mr. Franklins said.

Justin turned to see Mr. Franklins and the rest of the first-year boys waiting in the hall. Mr. Franklins, one of the party's chaperones, was dressed in a costume of all green.

"What are you supposed to be?" Luke, who was dressed as a cowboy, laughed. "Pajama man?"

"I'm a ninja," Justin said through gritted teeth. "What are you supposed to be, spokesman for fake leather?"

"I'm a cowboy." Luke said, aiming his silver-painted plastic gun at Justin.

"No aiming weapons at other students!" Mr. Franklins warned. "Or you'll have to stay here while the rest of us go to the party."

Luke lowered his gun as his eyes widened to the size of golf balls.

"It was just a joke," he rushed to say. "I wasn't going to shoot him!"

"But your toy gun could have gone off on accident and Justin could have gotten hurt," Mr. Franklins countered. "Just don't point it at anyone, okay?"

"Okay."

"Good. Now let's get to the party!"

With that, he gave a flourish of his lime green cloak and led them out of the dorms.

The auditorium

Like any school that has a Halloween party (though the Capes staff insists it's just a costume party, as to not offend anyone who thinks All Hallows' Eve is satanic), the decoration committee had covered the walls with orange, purple, green, and black streamers, placed rubber spiders in web-like gauze and hung them in the doorways, and placed miscellaneous pieces of plastic skeletons on the tables.

"Justin! Simon!" Eliza called as they entered the auditorium. She waved them over to where she, Annie, and Mary Anne were sitting.

"Nice costumes!" She said as they approached the table. "You guys look cool."

"Thanks!" Simon said, his cheeks growing pink beneath his mask.

"You're dressed as a... witch?" Justin said, eyeing her pointed hat.

"Yep," Eliza nodded. "The only thing I could think of to make my parents mad."

"Why do you want to make your parents mad?" Simon frowned.

Eliza eyed him warily.

"Because," she shrugged. She turned to Mary Anne, who dressed in a koala onesie. "Do they have cupcakes?"

"Yeah," Mary Anne nodded, causing the fuzzy ears of her onesie to flop over. "The kind that have rings in the frosting."

"Awesome," Eliza said, turning back to Justin. "Want to go grab one with me?"

"Sure," Justin shrugged.

"Cool," she turned to Simon. "We'll be right back."

Justin followed her into the mass of arriving third years, giving a perplexed Simon a shrug as they disappeared into the crowd.

"So why a ninja?" Eliza asked, joining the line at the refreshments table.

"I don't know, it seemed cool," Justin paused behind her in line. "Why a witch?"

"'Cause my stupid parents would hate it," Eliza said vaguely. "Not that they know. They only had enough money for Marian's costume. She wanted to be some roller derby girl, and skates don't come cheap."

"Then how'd you get your costume?" Justin frowned.

"My aunt paid for it," she dodged a kid in a construction worker's costume as he ran through the crowd.

"The one in Capsburg?" Justin asked, proud to have recalled that tidbit she'd shared with him on orientation day.

"That's the one," Eliza smiled fondly.

"Ah," Justin nodded. "Are you two close?"

"Kind of," She stepped forward with the line, eyeing the goodies laid out on the table. "I see her more than my other relatives and she's nice…"

"But?" Justin prompted.

"But I don't feel like we're close," she sighed. "It's not her fault, it's just… I only see her twice, maybe three times a year."

"I only see my aunts and uncles once every other year," Justin grabbed one of the paper plates and began piling goods onto it. "Not sure if that's because I grew up with the Willowses or if my family's just like that."

Eliza nodded, grabbing a cupcake that had a ghost ring stuck in its orange frosting.

"Eliza!" a voice called, cutting through the growing noise.

Bailey made her way towards them dressed as a princess.

"I love your dress!" Bailey gushed as she reached them. She glanced at Justin and frowned slightly. "Justin?"

"Yeah," he said, pulling his mask up.

"Hi!" She squeaked. "Nice ninja costume."

"Thanks, I like your princess… crown."

"That's from that series about the dragon catchers, right?" Eliza asked.

"Right!" Bailey beamed.

"She's got a cute smile," Justin thought, pulling his mask back down to cover his blush.

"I'm gonna go find Simon," he said, making his way back towards the table.

However, before he could get far, he spotted a familiar face in the crowd.

"Terrence!" he called to his brother, who was dressed as what Justin could only guess was supposed to be a bodyguard.

"Justin," his brother walked over to him, an easy smile lazily stretched across his face. "Nice costume."

"Thanks!" Justin said, surprised by the compliment.

"JASON!" Matt yelled, grabbing him from behind. "How's my bro's bro doing?"

"It's Justin, Matt," Peyton corrected, stepping forward to stand next to Terrence. He gave Justin an apologetic look as he tugged on the collar of his paint covered shirt.

"Pretty sure it's Jason," Matt said, releasing Justin from his grip.

"It's not," Terrence rolled his eyes.

"Whatever you say," Matt laughed, grabbing a nearby girl by her waist.

"Terrence," Justin said, trying to ignore the girl's peals of laughter. "Are you coming home for Thanksgiving?"

"Not sure yet," his brother shrugged.

"Man, you never visit your folks," Peyton shook his head. "You should go. You know they miss you."

"I visit for Christmas," Terrence said defensively.

"For three days," Justin pointed out.

"Then you spend the rest of the break at Matt's place," Peyton nodded. "You should visit home. For the whole break."

"I might," Terrence said, glaring at his friend.

"I've gotta go find my friend," Justin said, hoping to escape before things got more awkward. "I'll see you… later."

"See you around little man," Peyton nodded.

Terrence didn't say anything.

An hour later

Dancing in a ninja mask makes you really sweaty, really quick. Justin, however, was stubborn enough to keep the mask on a full hour before giving in to the fact that the mask was soaked.

"I'll be right back," he said to Simon, before rushing out of the auditorium, down the hall, and into the boy's bathroom.

Justin pulled off his mask and gloves and turned on the tap.

"Any news?" a voice said through the walls.

"Nothing," replied a second, a woman based on the pitch.

Justin carefully turned off the tap and dried his face with a paper towel.

"Well, something needs to be done!" the first person said. "Students are getting ill and we can't keep blaming it on allergies."

"It's being handled," the woman reminded him.

"But the culprit won't be caught this way!" The man said angrily, something about the way he pronounced 'caught' reminded Justin of someone.

"But they won't be able to harm any more students once the new security measures are in place."

"If it *is* Blackglycerin the new security measures won't matter!"

"Mr. Crain!" Justin realized. Mr. Crain often pronounced the t in words with a soft "tuh."

"Lower your voice," the woman said sternly. "One of the students might hear you."

Justin left as fast as he could, with only one thought in his mind.

"The teachers think it's him.*"*

Chapter Twenty-Three
Thanksgiving Break

"Do you hear anything?" Simon asked.

"Not yet," Justin replied.

"I don't think the meetings started yet," Eliza whispered. "They're just chatting."

"It's twelve thirty-seven, they should have started by now," Simon frowned.

"Wait," Eliza whispered. "I hear something!"

Yesterday (Friday), Amber had gone into Eliza's Minds class to relay a message to Mr. Fields. Eliza, wanting to get to the bottom of things, had read Mr. Fields's mind.

"He's pretty good at ESP blocking," Eliza told them when they'd met in the library that afternoon. "But I was able to hear two key pieces of information when he let his guard down; Tomorrow at eleven-thirty, Mr. Whitaker's office."

Justin pressed his ear to the wall of the hallway.

"Mr. Franklins, nice of you to join us," Mr. Whitaker said, his voice only slightly muffled by the wall.

"Sorry I'm late," Mr. Franklins apologized. "One of my students needed some help understanding the material that will be on the exam, so I was taking some time to explain it to him."

"Erik, could you please tell us why we're here?" a female voice said.

"Of course, Miranda," Mr. Whitaker replied. "We've received another note."

There were incoherent murmurs and groans from the teachers.

"What does this one say?" asked a low voice.

"*'Dear Mr. Whitaker and the teachers of Capes,'*" Mr. Whitaker read. "*'Your school has been the first of many that will be targeted. Now that I've seen how poorly you've responded to my attacks, I am forced to up my game. Your new security measures will do nothing to stop me, though they may at first delay my process. I will soon expose your school's…'*" Mr. Whitaker faltered. "Um…. Poor. *'Ways of keeping things under wraps to the public. Chaos will reign once again.'* They once again failed to sign it." Mr. Whitaker sighed.

"What are we going to do?" Mr. Crain asked in his croaky voice. Without being able to see the elderly man, Justin couldn't help but picture him as a frog.

"There might be nothing we can do," Ms. Núñez said.

"Well there has to be something!" Ms. Andromeda argued.

"We've kept an eye on the gate, we've upped the security for the kitchens, and we've searched the entire campus," a male voice reminded her. "What more can we do?"

"Mrs. Strong," Mr. Whitaker said, interrupting Ms. Andromeda's reply. "Do you have anything to add?"

The room was silent, Justin held his breath, waiting for the reply.

"I think," Mrs. Strong's soft voice said, barely audible through the wall. "That there is a disaster ahead. However, there is a chance it will end well."

"Did you have a vision?" Mr. Franklins asked.

"Just glimpses," Mrs. Strong said evasively.

"If any of you catch sight of anyone unfamiliar or anything suspicious, let me know immediately," Mr. Whitaker said. "We need to get to the bottom of this before it gets any worse."

"Justin," Eliza said, breaking his attention away from the conversation. "We need to go."

Justin gave a shaky nod and followed her and Simon to the stairwell.

After escaping to the gardens (the only vacant spot on the weekends) Justin began to speculate about the notes.

"If the teachers are the only ones who are supposed to know about the security changes," Justin wondered aloud. "Does that mean that Blackglycerin is one of them?"

"Not necessarily," Simon shrugged, picking one of the leaves off of a tree. "It could be one of the other staff."

"Technically," Eliza added. "It might not be any of the staff, he could have overheard it if he's living in the tunnels."

"But we saw no signs of someone living down there," Simon argued. "Just the footprint. Meaning he's most likely using the tunnel but not staying there."

Justin nodded.

"What do you think the first note said?" he asked.

"It might have been a ransom note," Simon suggested. "The second note almost made it seem like he had asked for something."

"Could be…" Eliza ceded. "But if that's true what does he want?"

A week later

As the cooler weather came as did the pumpkin spice flavored things in the cafeteria. The kitchen served pumpkin spice flavored coffees, cereals, and cookies for students to enjoy throughout the month of November. Despite the stricter searches of everything that came into the kitchen, more students were complaining of stomach pains and nausea, though whether that was because of poison or not no one knew because the medical staff was doing a good job of keeping everything under wraps.

"Kathryn went to the nurse's today," Eliza announced, sitting down on one of the garden benches.

"Did she have symptoms or not?" Simon asked, scribbling a note in his journal.

Eliza shook her head. "She says she felt sick, but I think she was just in her head about it."

"I'm pretty sure that's what most of the cases are," Simon nodded. "Fear turns everyone into hypochondriacs."

There was a pause between them.

"Are you guys heading home over break?" Simon asked.

"Yeah," Justin smiled, gazing at the dead leaves and evergreens surrounding them. "I get six days with my God family, then two with Pop Pop."

"Nice," Simon nodded appreciatively. "I leave Monday and get back Saturday."

"How about you, Eliza?" Justin asked before she could pick any more petals off of the wilting flowers.

"I'm going to be gone Saturday to Saturday," Eliza grimaced, dropping a petal on the ground and grinding it under her foot. "A whole week with my *lovely* family. On the bright side, I'll get to have my aunt's sweet potato casserole with candied pecans."

"My mom always makes that with mini marshmallows," Simon said, smiling at the thought. "But my favorite is mashed potatoes."

"You eat mashed potatoes on Thanksgiving?" Eliza said incredulously.

"You don't?" Justin laughed.

"Nope," Eliza held her head high.

"You're one of those people who likes pumpkin pie, aren't you?" Justin joked.

"You don't like pumpkin pie?!?" Eliza and Simon said in prime unison.

"It has a weird texture," Justin said defensively.

Eliza laughed, before glancing down at her Spanish worksheet. "Do either of you remember the conjugation?"

"You've already forgotten the song?" Simon frowned. "It's so easy."

"O, as, a, amos, an," Simon and Justin repeated.

"Nerds," Eliza smiled, copying down the endings. "And for E it's o, es, e, emos, en?"

"Right," Simon nodded.

Another week later

"Justin!" Will shouted, tackling him as he tried to enter the house.

"William!" Mrs. Willows scolded as the two boys fell to the floor. "Be gentle!"

"Sorry," Will smiled at her mischievously as he stood up.

"It's fine, Ma," Justin reassured her, trapping Will in a headlock.

Mrs. Willows rolled her eyes and smiled at the two of them.

"Lemme go!" Will grunted.

Justin released him from his hold.

"Terrence!" Justin turned to see a surprised Rose standing in the living room doorway.

"Hey, Ro," Terrence said, entering the house with a charlatan smile much different from the one Justin remembered. "How's it going?"

"It's okay," Rose shrugged modestly.

"We won eight of our ten games!" Will told them. "We beat the Dover Dingos, my mortal enemies."

"Like you have immortal enemies," Rose scoffed. "What are they? Time? Space?"

Everyone laughed as Will tried to think of a retort.

The next day

"So how's school?" Mr. Willows asked at breakfast.

"Well... there's a supervillain going around poisoning students," Justin thought to himself.

"Class, friends, anything?" Mrs. Willows prompted.

"Class is okay," Justin shrugged. "None of my teachers seem to hate me, and I like my classes okay."

"Which one is your favorite?" Mrs. Willows asked, grabbing another piece of bacon.

"Telekinesis and Portals," Justin thought.

"Probably Spanish," he said, because, in all honesty, it was the easiest and Ms. Núñez was genuinely nice.

"Terrence?" Mrs. Willows asked.

Terrence shrugged, not looking up from his plate.

"My karate classes aren't bad," he said broodingly.

"You get to take karate?" Will asked.

Terrence gave him a small smile.

"Yeah, it's pretty cool," he said, his eyes sparkling the way Eliza's did when she talked about her sisters. "The chic that teaches it is pretty ba-" he faltered at Mr. Willow's glare. "Pretty cool."

Rose rolled her eyes at Will's snickering.

"Are you enjoying the kids in your grade?" Mrs. Willows asked, obviously wanting to distract her giggling children. "Made any friends?"

"A couple," Justin nodded. "Most of the guys in my dorm are okay. I mostly hang out with my friends Eliza and Simon, they're both really cool."

A part of Justin wished he could tell them about his and his friends' powers, but the rule Ms. Ties made sure they knew was that *under no circumstances* do you tell a Norm about your or anyone else's powers.

"Wonderful," Mrs. Willows said, smiling politely. "Terrence, how are Matt, Peyton, and Chris?"

"Matt and Peyton are good," Terrence said, fixing her with a bored stare. "I haven't talked to Chris."

"Why not?" Mrs. Willows frowned. "I thought you guys were good friends?"

"He kind of withdrew from the group when we split into smaller dorms," Terrence said bluntly, staring at his meatloaf.

Justin recalled the group of chanting boys from his first night at Capes.

"What made him want to leave the group?" Justin wondered.

"So what's it like having Terrence as a brother?" Ray Kindle's question rang in his head.

Wednesday

Mrs. Willows had arranged a pre-Thanksgiving picnic at a local park with some of Justin's friends. The plan was to bring a potluck of snacks and let the children play for a couple hours before the parents had to head home to start preparing for Thanksgiving.

"Sam!" Justin yelled, racing toward his friend.

"Justin!" Sam said, waving him over to where he and their friend Franklin stood.

"How have you been?" Justin panted.

"Pretty good," Sam smiled. "Mr. Plumes was sick for two weeks and we had a sub."

"He wouldn't stop talking about it!" Franklin groaned.

"So how's life at your hoity-toity boarding school?" Sam asked in a bad British accent.

"It's fine," Justin bit back a brag. "I've made a couple of friends and the classes are okay."

"Any of the teachers as bad as Mr. Plumes?" Franklin asked.

"My… History teacher, Mr. Crain, is kind of grumpy," Justin admitted. "And my science teacher hands out too much homework."

Sam and Franklin nodded sympathetically.

Justin noticed the equipment at their feet.

"Wanna play some football?" he asked.

"Yes!" Sam grabbed a football from the pile and ran as fast as he could in the other direction. "Go long!"

Thanksgiving day

"Terrence, can you cut these for me?" Mrs. Willows asked, holding a knife and a peeled potato for him to take.

"Sure, Ma," Terrence said, taking them from her.

"Thank you," Mrs. Willows sighed, patting his cheek. "Rose, can you peel the rest of the potatoes?"

She gestured towards the remaining four potatoes.

"Mo-om." Rose groaned.

"Please and thank you!" Mrs. Willows turned to check the oven.

"Come on, Ro," Terrence waved for her to join him at the counter. "When we finish we can partake in our tradition of helping make the pie…"

"And eating the whip cream," Rose smiled, hopping up from her seat at the table.

"Justin," Mrs. Willows said. "Could you watch the water in this pot and let me know when it's boiling?"

"Yeah," he said, abandoning his math homework to stand by the stove.

"Thank you, sweetie," she said, turning to work on the stuffing.

An hour and a half later the stuffing was put in a bowl, the turkey basted, the potatoes mashed, the green beans strained, the sweet potato casserole and the rolls removed from the oven, the pies left to cool, and the cranberry sauce plopped from its can with a satisfying "schloop" sound.

As soon as they finished saying grace, the mad dash to grab the best of the feast began. Justin, now eating the biggest roll, realized how much he'd missed home cooked meals. Sure, the food at Capes was good, but it wasn't the same as when Mr. or Mrs. Willows made it.

"It's really good!" Justin said between bites.

"Thank you," Mrs. Willows smiled. "I couldn't have done it without you guys."

"Yeah, you could have," Terrence laughed.

"Mom, we can't cook," Rose shrugged.

"Speak for yourself," Mr. Willows said. "I make a mean mac and cheese."

"And I make good brownies," Terrence said.

"You should make some before you leave!" Rose said, accidentally flinging mashed potatoes at her brother.

"Hey!" Will said, loading his fork for retaliation.

"I'll try and make some for you before we leave," Terrence promised.

"Good," Rose smiled. "That makes up for abandoning us so early."

"We won't be gone long," Justin pointed out. "We come right back for Christmas break."

"That's true, and then we get to stay for two more weeks," Terrence added, to Justin's surprise.

"He's not going to Matts for Christmas break!" Justin realized.

"Still," Rose grumbled, her lower lip protruding in a pout.

"Could have been worse," Justin shrugged. "We could have left right now and ended up missing family game night."

"Sounds like a win-win to me," Will said, his mouth once again full of food. "Either way you guys leave."

"William!" Mrs. Willows exclaimed.

"I'm kidding," Will protested.

That night

Terrence and Rose won the first three games of game night, Mr. and Mrs. Willows won the next one, and Justin and Will won the last two.

"Alright, you two," Mr. WIllows pointed at the twins. "Off to bed."

"Aw, Dad," Rose pleaded. "Ten more minutes?"

"You're just jealous you didn't win, Dad," Will said.

"Not at all," Mrs. Willows laughed. "I just don't want two grumpy kids tomorrow, you've got practice."

As Rose and Will headed upstairs, Justin moved from the floor to the armchair, curling up in a fetal position to get comfortable. Terrence stayed sitting on the floor, muscles tensed, like a cat sensing a storm brewing, as he stared at the discarded napkins from their brownies.

"I've been meaning to ask, how was your summer, Terrence?" Mrs. Willows asked.

Terrence looked warily.

"Fine," he said softly. "The Reynolds's let me accompany them to the beach for a week…"

"You could have come with us on our beach trip," Mr. Willows said pointedly.

"Nathaniel…" Mrs. Willows warned.

"I'm just saying he could have visited," Mr. Willows said, holding his hands up in surrender.

Terrence glared at the carpet.

"Well, transportation has been a problem," Mrs. Willows said. "but maybe next year..."

"You know what? I'm going to bed," Terrence said abruptly.

Mr. and Mrs. Willows watched in silence as he left the room.

"So how's the undercover life?" Mrs. Willows asked Justin as Terrence's footsteps retreated upstairs.

"Good," Justin nodded. "Apparently I'm pretty powerful... I have a really rare ability."

"With your mother's talents, I'm not surprised," Mrs. Willows smiled fondly. "Are you good at using any of them yet?"

"Kind of…" Justin shrugged. "But I could be better."

"At least you're honest." Mrs. Willows nodded encouragingly.

"Yeah," Justin smiled. "No matter how special I think I am, I have to remember that one of my friends is the smartest kid in our grade and the other one is the most powerful, so I'm being humbled."

Mr. and Mrs. Willows laughed.

The next day

Mr. Lains was waiting for them on the sidewalk when they stepped out of the phone booth.

"There's my two growing grandsons," he chuckled, pulling them into a hug.

"Hi, Pop Pop," Justin smiled.

"Hey, Papa," Terrence said, pulling away from the hug to grab his bags.

"I know you two are probably full from yesterday's feast," Mr. Lains said, taking one of Terrence's bags from him. "However, there's a diner I'm dying to show you. They have amazing milkshakes."

The Dairy Parlor

The Dairy Parlor looked like something right out of the nineteen fifties. From its blue booths and checkerboard tiled floor to its dime-operated table jukeboxes, everything about the place screamed old school. However, you could tell it was a frequented and well-loved establishment from the cracks in the vinyl upholstery and numbers that had been worn away on the mini jukebox.

"Two strawberry milkshakes, one chocolate," their waitress, Paula, said, placing their drinks on the table.

"A hamburger for you," she set the plate in front of Mr. Lains. "A chili dog for the young man and a grilled cheese for you. Lemme know if you need anything else."

She hummed along to the song playing overhead as she walked away, her blonde ponytail bobbing to the beat.

"Have you been to Cafton before?" Mr. Lains asked Terrence.

"I've been on the weekends, but I've never come here," Terrence said between bites.

"Not many kids do, they probably think they can't afford it," Mr. Lains said.

Terrence's phone started buzzing. He picked up his phone and frowned.

"I've got to take this," he said, sliding out of the booth.

"So how's your search going?" Mr. Lains inquired as soon as Terrence was out of earshot.

"Not well," Justin admitted. "We overheard the teachers talking about a ransom note."

"What does he want for his ransom?" Mr. Lains asked, his eyes growing wide.

"We don't know," Justin sighed. "But he's going to keep targeting students until he gets it."

Outside of Capes

"Here you go," Mr. Lains said, parking his car in front of the path to Capes. "Y'all sure you wanna walk by yourselves?"

"We're sure," Terrence said firmly, hopping out of the car.

"Okay, then," Mr. Lains said, his smile suddenly forced. "I'll hopefully see y'all soon."

"See you soon, Pop Pop," Justin promised, rushing to catch up with his brother.

"Hey!" someone called from behind him. "Justin!"

Justin turned to see Bailey walking towards him, followed people he assumed were her older siblings.

"Hey, Bailey," he smiled.

"You just got back from your Godparents' house?" She asked, noticing his bags.

"No," he shook his head. "We left Friday morning and spent the weekend with my grandfather."

"Fun!" Bailey nodded. "My family lives just outside of Cafton, so we're walking back. Oh!" she gave him an apologetic look. "Sorry, let me introduce my siblings. This is Ashley, Julie, Thomas, and Teresa."

Her siblings each waved as she said their names. Ashley, the oldest, looked the most like Bailey with long blonde hair pulled back into a ponytail and green eyes identical to Bailey's. Julie was a little shorter than Ashley and only a couple inches taller than Bailey. Her hair, blonde like her sisters, was in a pixie cut. Justin assumed Thomas and Teresa were twins because they looked the most alike out of their siblings. They both had dark blond hair, hazel eyes, and similar smirks.

"Hi," Justin said shyly.

"Did you enjoy your Thanksgiving, Justin?" Julia asked.

"Yeah," Justin nodded. "I got to spend some time with my old friends and my God siblings and eat a lot of pecan pie."

"We had pecan pie too!" Bailey said excitedly. "We also had pizza three of the six nights we were home, which was funny cause Daddy hates pizza."

"He likes it better than the food at Capes," Ashley pointed out.

"Who wouldn't when the food at Capes could kill you?" Teresa joked.

"I think it's Mr. Crain," Thomas said seriously. So seriously, Justin wouldn't have been able to tell it was a joke if Teresa hadn't smirked. "I think he's trying to do away with his least favorite students."

"Thomas, don't joke," Ashley scolded.

"Yeah, you might be next," Teresa laughed.

Ashley rolled her eyes, scanning her I.D. on the gate's keypad to let them onto campus.

"Well, I think Mr. Crain is too nice to kill students," Bailey said seriously as they approached the main building. "I'll see you later, Justin," she said, following her sisters towards the girls' dorm.

"See you!" Justin said, making his way to the boy's dorm.

Simon was sitting on his bed when Justin entered the room

"You're back!" he said.

"Nah, this is just a hologram," Justin laughed.

"Oh," Simon nodded. "Wow, impressive. Tell the real Justin that I *totally* didn't prop my feet up on his bed."

"Ew," Justin giggled as he grimaced.

Chapter Twenty-Four
The Fight

Distinct Abilities was finally covering Electric Manipulation.

"Electric Manipulation, like a lot of rare abilities, hasn't been seen in a couple of years," Mrs. Strong announced to the class. "So it's a treat to get to learn about it. Like other manipulation powers, Electric Manipulation is based on emotions. The better the user can control their emotions, the better they can control the ability. Justin, have you been able to use the ability at all?"

Justin had a sudden flashback of the blue light in his bathroom before he'd left for Capes.

"Kind of…" he said modestly.

"Okay," Mrs. Strong nodded encouragingly. "How about we give it a try?"

She pulled an artificial candle out of the pocket of her cardigan and handed it to him.

"Try focusing on the candle and turn it on," she sat on the floor in front of him, her gaze focused on the plastic, unlit flame.

"Okay," he stared at the candle, wondering if he could achieve the task in record time.

After five minutes, it seemed he couldn't.

"Sometimes nothing happens," Mrs. Strong said calmly as if the five minutes he'd wasted were of no concern. "You can try again if you want or we can move on to how the ability works and can be defeated."

"I wanna try again," Justin said, trying to ignore the quiver in his hands.

"Okay," Mrs. Strong nodded again.

Justin looked at Eliza. She gave him a tiny nod and mouthed *"focus."*

After one more look at the faux candle, Justin closed his eyes.

He remembered playing football with his friends in the park. The fear he'd felt when exploring the tunnels. The way Eliza talked about her family. The laugh Rose emitted when Terrence, laughing just as hard, had put a dollop of whip cream on her nose. The way Bailey had blushed when they were talking.

There were screams.

Justin opened his eyes as the classroom lights flickered back on.

"Well..." Mrs. Strong said, standing to her feet. "We'll have to work on using the ability on a more controlled scale, but good job!"

Justin felt his face heat up and was sure his face was a blotchy mess. The smirk Eliza gave him as she silently applauded only confirmed that suspicion.

Three days later

"Find anything suspicious when you talked to Mr. Franklins?" Simon asked Justin in a hushed tone.

Justin gave only the slightest shake of his head as he continued to pretend to listen to Luke's rant about... something (once again, Justin didn't know what the rant was about because he was only pretending to listen).

"That was uncalled for!" a voice called from across the cafeteria.

The room fell quiet as everyone turned to find the source of the outburst. It wasn't hard to find. A girl with dark hair stood, glaring at the boy across from her, who Justin couldn't see through her.

"Then don't talk about my life as if you know me," the boy said calmly.

The voice sounded familiar, but it was too hard to tell who it was because he was on the other side of the room.

"It's not you!" the girl yelled.

Lola. Justin remembered. *She's in art club.*

"You're better than this, Terrence."

Justin felt as if he'd been set on fire then doused in ice water.

"You don't know me," Terrence said angrily.

"I do," Lola argued. "Or at least I did. You're better than this."

"Leave," Terrence said with such force that Justin himself almost got up to exit the room.

"Don't you use persuasion on me!" Lola said, her voice seething with poison. "'Cause I'll just use it on you!"

"Try me," Terrence said, standing to her height.

Lola leaned towards him and said something inaudible to the listeners.

Terrence stared at her defiantly for a second, before crumpling to the floor.

Justin was on his feet before the teachers reached him.

"You. Principal's office. Now," one of the teachers said to Lola.

Lola turned and left without giving Terrence a second glance.

Study Hall

"Mrs. Rodriguez?" Eliza asked.

"Yes, dear?" Mrs. Rodriguez said, glancing up from her computer.

"Have..." Eliza paused, frowning.

Out of the three of them, Eliza was the best at playing innocent. She said it was *"people underestimating her,"* but Justin knew it was because she was good at hiding her emotions.

"Why did you and Mr. Rodriguez start working here?" she cocked her head to the side and made her eyes wider, giving herself an innocent look.

"Well..." Mrs. Rodriguez tried to suppress her smile. "We wanted to find a place where we could work together and still have time to spend with our children and Capes offered that. Our kids are grown now, but we still enjoy the free time."

"When did you start working here?" Eliza asked.

"About..." her fingers twitched as she did the math. "Twenty-five years."

"Wow," Eliza nodded. "Does that include any... long breaks from work?"

"Teachers would need to take long breaks if they were... you know leading riots," Simon said. *"So maybe we should ask the staff if they've ever taken long breaks."*

"Oh no," Mrs. Rodriguez laughed. "Though we're not *technically* teachers, we enjoy the job. We usually wait until summer to take breaks. Last summer we went on a cruise to the Bahamas."

Eliza nodded, listening to Mrs. Rodriguez as she began to retell the story.

Art club

Justin approached Lola as soon as art ended.

"Um… hi," he said, grabbing her attention away from her friend. "I'm Justin… Terrence's brother."

"I know who you are Justin," she sighed, wincing slightly. "I'm sorry about what I did to your brother."

"Thanks…" Justin said, trying not to show his confusion. "What *did* you do to him?"

"We both can bend people to our will," Lola explained. "So I convinced him to pass out."

"Why?" Justin breathed.

She studied his face for a second.

"Your brother and I were good friends," she shrugged, turning to inspect her painting. "Recently, he's been making some choices I don't think are really him. Out of anger, I reacted poorly."

"What choices did he make?"

"It's not my gossip to share," she said bluntly. "I am sorry though. He didn't deserve a mild concussion, even if he was being a jerk."

"He's not always a jerk," Justin said quietly.

"I know," Lola sighed. "That's why it makes me so sad when he acts like one. Your brother's a good person Justin, he's just really lost right now."

December fifth

"Breakfast ends in thirty minutes," Mr. Franklins said to the last of the stragglers in the room. "And happy birthday, Simon."

"Thank you!" Simon smiled as Justin turned to give him an incredulous look.

"Why didn't you tell me today was your birthday?" Justin asked.

"It's not a big deal," Simon shrugged.

"Of course it is!" Justin said, exasperatedly. "I'll get you something, I promise."

"You don't have to," Simon said, blushing.

"But I'm going to."

Lunch

"So... he can come?" Justin said, double-checking for anxiety's sake.

"He can come," Mrs. Strong repeated. "But just for today!"

"Awesome!" Justin turned to run down the hall... then stopped and turned back around. "Thank you."

"Of course," Mrs. Strong said as Justin raced back into the cafeteria.

"Where were you?" Eliza asked as soon as Justin sat down at the table.

"In the hall," Justin said. He turned to Simon. "I got you something."

"You didn't have t-" Simon objected.

"Don't worry, it didn't cost me anything..." Justin paused. "That came out wrong."

"It's fine," Simon laughed, abandoning his fork in his excitement. "What is it?"

"I got you a one-time visit to the best class at Capes."

Distinct Abilities

"Welcome class," Miss Andromeda said, addressing the class as they settled into their seats. "As you can see, Simon will be joining us today for his birthday."

Justin led a round of applause and "happy birthdays" as Simon blushed.

"Anyways," Mrs. Strong said as everyone quieted. "Today we will be taking a look at Eliza's ability to look into the future. Now, future seers can divine the future in many ways. One may have a prophetic dream, another could simply reach forward into their mind and grab a scene from the future. A third might simply see glimpses, like a flash of lightning from the future," she paused. "Of course there's also the matter of prophecies, but that's for another day."

Several kids sighed. Justin would have been as disappointed if Eliza hadn't already told him a plethora of facts about prophecies.

"It's rare for one futureseer to be able to divine the future using more than two methods," Mrs. Strong continued. "However, it isn't unheard of. The one hard thing about being a futureseer is bringing the visions forth."

Michael raised his hand.

"Yes, Mr. Hunt?" Miss Andromeda nodded at him.

"So, what are you going to do to get Eliza to see something?" he asked.

"Well, Mrs. Strong," she gestured to the older teacher. "Is going to try to prompt it out of Miss Thistle."

"Eliza, if you would please stand," Mrs. Strong suggested.

Eliza, who until that moment had kept her gaze stubbornly set on the floor, stood and stood before Mrs. Strong in the middle of the circle. Mrs. Strong held out her ring adorned hands for Eliza to take.

"You're a mind reader, correct?" Mrs. Strong asked as Eliza gingerly placed her hands atop of her palms.

Eliza nodded, her hands quivering.

"She doesn't like reading someone's thoughts," Justin realized.

"Would you like to be the person intruding on someone's private thoughts?" he argued with himself.

"Now, I'm going to recall an event. I want you to try and see the picture I'm painting," Mrs. Strong gave Eliza's hands a gentle squeeze. "The more details you see the more likely you'll be able to divine from the future."

Eliza took a deep breath and nodded.

"This part won't be interesting to watch," Miss Andromeda warned. "But, if she has a vision, it will be the most interesting thing to happen in class all semester."

"And," Mrs. Strong added. "The quieter you are the sooner we get results."

Everyone's whispering fell silent as they watched Mrs. Strong and Eliza with wide eyes.

Mrs. Strong's eyelids fell closed and Eliza's gaze hardened as she tried to see whatever scene Mrs. Strong was playing for her in her mind.

Justin leaned forward in his seat as Eliza's eyes slowly became a glassy bronze color and her grip on Mrs. Strong's hands tightened.

Miss Andromeda raised a hand, effectively silencing Kimba's question before she could even open her mouth.

Eliza gasped, blinking the last of the bronze color out of her eyes. Mrs. Strong released Eliza's hands and grasped her elbows as Eliza slouched forward.

"I'm fine," Eliza said as Justin and Simon moved to help her. "Just a little dizzy."

"That happens," Mrs. Strong nodded. "Justin, could you help Eliza to her seat?"

Justin nodded and helped her walk to her chair.

"Well," Mrs. Strong said, addressing the bewildered students. "As you can probably gather from Eliza's reaction, she had some sort of vision."

Eliza nodded, grabbing her water bottle from her bag.

"If it's nothing too personal, would you mind sharing with the class?" Miss Andromeda asked.

Eliza shrugged, taking a swig from her water bottle.

"It was more of a glimpse than a coherent scene," Eliza paused, thinking for a minute. "But I think Sandwich Wednesday is going to be great this week."

That night: the library

"So what did you *really* see?" Justin asked as soon as Hannah, one of Amber's friends, left the room.

Eliza took her time finishing the sentence she was writing.

"Do you remember Obstacle Course Day?" she asked.

"Yeah, why?" Justin frowned.

"After Force Fields, you saw someone in the hallway?" she prompted.

"There were a lot of people in the hallway," Justin pointed out.

"Yeah, but one of them was a stranger," she urged.

Justin frowned, trying to retrieve the hazy memory.

"Maybe…" he said. "Why, what did you see?"

"I saw you remembering who you saw," she shrugged.

"But I don't know who I saw," Justin protested.

"But you will," Eliza insisted. "You just have to try."

Justin sighed. "Fine."

"Good," Eliza sat up a little straighter. "Now try and remember as much as you can."

"I'll try," he said, closing his eyes.

"Great job class!" Miss Drills said as she put out the rest of the fire. "That was the best run I've seen any first-year class do."

The bell rang and they ran from the room as quickly as their tired legs could bear to run. Kyle was in front of him, Luke to his right, and Bailey to his left, her blonde curls bouncing as she walked beside him.

They headed for the stairwell… where someone was exiting.

Justin tried to focus on his face, his brain buzzing from the effort.

The stranger bumped into Kyle, drawing Justin's attention to him.

He looked about twenty-seven, maybe older. His hair was dark blond and mostly covered by a red hat, the few strands Justin could see were greasy. He was bulky and dressed in a white tee and khaki pants.

Justin opened his eyes.

"I remembered!"

Three weeks later

After reviewing their list of all the staff at Capes and coming up empty, they checked the seniors.

"Maybe one of them was absent?" Simon suggested.

"Three weeks in a row?" Eliza said incredulously. "We only get fifty minutes for lunch, that's not enough time to waste on going out to eat every day."

"Besides, there's no way he was a student," Justin said, arguing his point once again. "He was a graduate at least."

"It was probably a disguise," Simon said for the fifth time that day. "Who's to say he won't change appearance again?"

"It's too much hassle to have to change your appearance that many times," Eliza said, once again changing part of the stripe in her hair to prove her point. "We'll have to check the logs of who comes on and off the property to get any kind of new clue."

"We can do that?" Justin frowned.

"Probably," she shrugged.

Third floor

"We cause a distraction while Simon checks the computer.... Right?" Justin double-checked.

"Right," Eliza confirmed.

Simon stopped just ahead of them.

"Shoot," he muttered.

"What?" Justin whispered.

"Michael's in there," he whispered back, pointing towards Valerie's office.

"What do we do?" Eliza asked.

Before any of them could come up with an answer, Michael stepped out of the office.

He brightened when he noticed them and made his way to where they stood in front of the stairwell.

"Hey, guys!" he smiled. "I was just doing some…"

He glanced behind him.

"Recon," He whispered.

"Recon?" Simon frowned.

"Yeah," Michael continued to whisper. "There's a group of students that are trying to investigate what's been going on. You know, the alleged poisoning."

"So what are you doing here?" Eliza asked.

"Seeing if anyone who doesn't work here came here," he shrugged. "They sent me because I'm a first-year and unlikely to be suspected of being a part of an investigation."

"Because they wouldn't take us seriously," Justin said slowly.

"Yeah," Michael smiled and nodded again. "Anyways, it worked! Valerie told me that no one came or left in the past two months other than staff."

"Awesome," Eliza frowned at him. "Bye."

She turned and left.

"Wait!" Michael called. "Weren't you coming up here for something?"

"Nope, just taking laps," Justin said jokingly, following Eliza down the stairs.

"I- Sorry." he heard Simon say, as his footsteps followed his friends.

"Valerie would have never given us a real answer," Eliza said as they exited the building. "We're too young to need a real answer, so why would she give it to us?"

"So there's no real answer," Simon realized.

"There's no real answer," Justin agreed.

Chapter Twenty-Five
It's Beginning to Look a Lot Like… Fighting.

"Pencil's down."

Justin, despite his earlier confidence, was ninety-nine point nine percent sure that he had gotten at least half of the multiple-choice questions wrong. If you think regular history is hard, you should try taking Hero History.

"Remember," Mr. Franklins said, collecting their completed tests. "There's always time next semester to raise your grade. And if you fail a test, you can do make-up work over break."

He winked at Justin as he grabbed his test.

Lunch

"I think I failed," Simon fretted.

"If you think you failed then the rest of us are doomed," Jerry, one of Luke's friends, pointed out.

"You didn't fail Simon," Eliza rolled her eyes. "You're just overthinking it."

Simon nodded distractedly, clearly not reassured, and picked at his sandwich.

"Guess what!" Luke suddenly said.

"What?" asked half the table.

"My sister's going to be visiting for the holidays!" he announced, bouncing in his seat. "She's super cool."

"We always go to our grandparent's house," Bailey said. "And this year Israel, my oldest brother is coming from San Francisco."

120 Two Bridges Street

A holly wreath greeted them as they arrived at the Willows household.

"Home again, home again," Mr. Willows said.

"Jiggity jig," Justin and Terrence said, listlessly finishing the phrase.

"You're back!" Will yelled, flinging open the front door.

"William!" Mrs. Willows called from the kitchen. "Let them into the house before you attack them."

Will rolled his eyes and stepped back, gesturing down the hall.

"Welcome to our hum-bull a-bode," he said lazily.

"How was your birthday?" Justin asked as Terrence and Mr. Willows laughed.

"Amazing!" Will smiled, his eyes lighting up. "Tyler and Dillon spent the night and-"

"It was *not* amazing," Rose groaned as they entered the kitchen. "They were so loud, Taylor, Natalie, and I couldn't hear ourselves think."

"You mean gossip," Will poked her in the shoulder.

"Stop," Rose complained.

"It was quite the night," Mr. Willows nodded, removing his glasses to run a hand over his eyes.

"I bet," Terrence nodded, making his way upstairs to his room.

"I brought you gifts," Justin said, pulling his backpack off his shoulder to get two packages out of it.

"Gimme!" Will said, lunging for the gifts.

"William," Mrs. Willows called from the kitchen.

"This one's yours," Justin said, handing him a green-wrapped object. "And this one's yours." He handed Rose the other gift.

"Thanks," Rose said, gingerly opening her present as Will tore into his.

"Cool!" Will said, ripping the plastic off of his new game controller.

"Oh wow," Rose smiled, holding up her new notebook and pens for her father to see. "Thank you, Justin!"

"You're welcome. And happy late birthday."

"We're going for dinner Saturday to celebrate as a family," Mrs. Willows said.

"We're going to Pizza Pemoli's!" Will said, pumping his fist in the air.

Pizza Pemoli's

"Two pepperoni pan pizzas, a Pemoli's special, and an order of bacon-wrapped pepper poppers," their waiter said as his colleagues set their food on their table.

"It all looks wonderful," Mrs. Willows gushed, eyeing her Pemoli's special (a salad and calzone). "Thank you, Alex."

"Of course," the waiter smiled, placing the pepper poppers on the table. "Enjoy."

The Willows-Strikes family dug into their food as the table lapsed into silence.

After wolfing down three slices, Will looked at his mother and announced. "I wanna go to the arcade."

"The rest of us are still eating," Mr. Willows said.

"But I'm done," Will pouted.

"I could go with him," Justin offered.

"You're only two years older than me," Will said, his face scrunched up in disgust. "I should be able to go by myself."

"I can go with them," Terrence said, setting down his slice.

"You don't have to if you don't want to," Mrs. Willows said, trying to disguise her obvious relief.

"No, it's fine," Terrence insisted, pushing back his chair. "I really don't mind."

"Let's go!" Will shouted, jumping up.

"Inside voice," Mr. Willows said as Will led Justin and Terrence towards the arcade zone.

"One rule," Terrence said, pointing at Will. "You're not allowed to spend more than an hour trying to get something out of the claw machine. Ten minutes tops. I'm not going through that jazz again."

"I don't wanna play the claw game," Will chirped. "I wanna play the zombie killing game!"

"Well…" Terrence shrugged. "Ma didn't say no."

"Awesome!" Will yelled, running towards the game.

"If he gets nightmares Ma will kill you," Justin told his brother.

"It's her money that's paying for the game," he shrugged again.

"Zom-Bees!" Will yelled, grabbing the plastic gun as the game began.

"For every zombie you kill, I'll give you one of my tickets," Terrence promised.

"But you don't have any tickets," Justin frowned.

"Not yet," Terrence agreed. "But I'm a skiiball wizard."

"I'm up to six!" Will announced as the game became eerily quiet.

BAM! A zombie came out of nowhere with a loud bang.

Justin jumped as the room went dark.

"What the-" Terrence said as the lights flickered back on.

"Yes!" Will cheered. "The game didn't restart!"

Terrence gave Justin a wide-eyed glance.

"Was that you?" he whispered.

Justin continued to force himself to take deep breaths. "I think so."

Terrence swore.

"You should go back to the table," he said. "I'll talk to you about this later, okay?"

"Okay," Justin mumbled, trying to not take it personally.

"You're back soon," Mrs. Willows observed as Justin sat back down at the table.

"There wasn't anything I wanted to play," Justin lied half-heartedly.

Mrs. Willows studied his face but didn't reply.

That night: The Willows' house

"Justin, could you give us a minute?" Mrs. Willows asked.

He turned to Terrence, who gave him a solemn nod.

"Sure," Justin said, turning to head upstairs.

"I didn't want to, okay?" Terrence's voice echoed upstairs.

"Why not?" Mrs. Willows' voice was harder to hear from upstairs.

"Because!" Terence sounded exasperated. "It doesn't feel like home anymore."

Justin heard a door open and looked down the hall. Rose was standing in the doorway of her room.

"Is that why you sent Justin back to the table?" Mrs. Willows asked. "Because he isn't a part of your crowd?"

"No, Ma, there was a reason for that."

"Well, it better be a pretty good one," Mr. Willows said.

"I'm not doing this with you," Terrence said, his footsteps approaching the stairs.

Justin and Rose hurried to close their doors.

Justin sank onto his bed as Terrence's footsteps came to a stop.

There was a knock and Terrence opened the door.

"You okay?" Terrence asked, closing the door behind him.

"Me?" Justin said incredulously. "You're the one in trouble!"

"Yeah, well… I was expecting a fight," Terrence shrugged, sitting next to his brother on the bed. "You, however, caused a blackout in half a building."

Justin sheepishly looked down at his hands.

"I don't know how I did it," He admitted.

"I think that game scared you a bit more than you let on, Terrence said, rubbing his thumb over the palm of his hand. "I did that once. My friend, Chris, jumped out from behind a door and I almost set him on fire."

"So how do you keep yourself from doing something like that?" Justin asked.

"Depends on…" Terrence paused. "What are all your powers?"

"Force fields, telekinesis, portals, and electric manipulation," Justin listed.

"Okay," Terrence nodded. He paused, taking a moment to think. "For telekinesis, try using a little bit on little things each day. Obviously, make sure no one is around if you're not at school. Same thing with portals. Use a little each day, make sure you're not seen. For force fields, set aside a day to practice so you don't glitch and for electric manipulation try subtly messing with electronics. Make something turn on a second early or a second late."

"Yeah, okay," Justin nodded. "I can do that."

"Don't worry," Terrence put his arm around his brother. "You're not going to be discovered. Everything's going to be okay."

Justin didn't say anything. It wasn't himself he was worried about.

Missouri

Grandma and Grandpa Willows were fantastic gift-givers. Doesn't matter if you're their kid, grandkid, adopted grandkid, mailman, or third-grade science teacher, each gift had the same amount of thought put into it.

"This one's for William, this is Rose's," Grandma Willows said, distributing the gifts. "Here's Terrence's, this one is for Nathaniel and Willene, and this one is Justin's."

She winked as she handed Justin his package.

Will had ripped into his gift before Justin could even decide how to open his.

"Cool!" Will said, holding up his new cleats.

Justin finished opening his new video games.

"Woah!" He gaped at Grandma and Grandpa WIllows. "Thank you!"

"Of course!" Grandma Willows smiled.

Rose had already started reading the first book in her new box set as Will tried on his new shoes.

"Again, thank you so much," Terrence said as he began trying to set up his new laptop.

"No problem," Grandpa Willows said. "We thought we could try to bribe you into visiting us more."

The adults chuckled as Terrence shifted uncomfortably in his seat.

"I think this needs to charge first," Terrence mumbled, releasing the power button.

"Lemme try," Justin said.

Terrence placed the laptop in his lap. Justin held his finger over the power button and focused. The screen flickered to life as the lights in the room dimmed by a fraction.

"Yikes," Mrs. Willows frowned. "It must be about to rain if a cloud is covering that much sun that quickly."

"Good job," Terrence muttered to Justin under his breath.

Christmas day

After stockings were emptied, presents opened, and lunch was eaten, the Willows-Strikes household took a trip to the St. Allens Home for Mental Wellness.

"Well if it isn't the Willows family," Sandra Willes, the owner of St. Allens, greeted them. "Merry Christmas, it's wonderful to see y'all!"

"Merry Christmas, Sandra!" Mrs. Willows smiled. "We're here to see Gerald and Clarissa."

"Of course!" Ms. Willes nodded, typing something into her computer. "They're in room 320."

"Thank you, Sandra," Mrs. Willows said, leading the way to the elevator.

"No problem!" Ms. Willes called after them.

Justin was glad Will was distracted by his new game as they crowded into the elevator. Will was notorious for pressing as many elevator buttons as he could before his parents noticed. Without Will's shenanigans, they made their way to the second floor in silence.

Mr. Strikes was sitting in a chair by the window, as he usually was when they entered the room. Mrs. Strikes was looking upward, her gaze fixed on the light fixture above her.

"Clarissa," Mrs. Willows said, gently touching her friend on the arm.

Mrs. Strikes jerked her head towards her.

"Willene!" she gasped. "Gerald, it's Willene!"

Mr. Strikes turned his head away from the window but didn't look at any of them.

"Hey, Mamma." Terrence said quietly.

"Hello dear," she walked towards him and patted him on the arm. "Lovely to see you."

Justin set down the tinfoil-covered tray they'd brought on the bedside table as Will flopped down into a nearby chair, eyes still glued to his game.

Mr. Strikes muttered something from the corner.

"We brought cookies," Mrs. Willows announced as Mrs. Strikes made her way back towards her.

"Lemon sugar?" Mrs. Strikes asked, her nails digging into Mrs. Willows's arm.

"Peanut butter," Rose said, unwrapping the tray to hand her one.

Mrs. Strikes took the cookie and immediately dropped it.

"Hot hot," she mumbled, rubbing her hand. "Bad things bad guy hot hot."

Justin and Terrence shared a startled glance as Mrs. Willows bent down to pick up the cookie.

That night

"Well, that was a pleasant trip," Mrs. Willows remarked as they got home. She turned to Terrence. "I'm sure you're glad you got to see your parents again."

"Yeah..." he nodded. "It was... nice... But at the same time it hurts, you know?"

"Yeah, I know," Mrs. Willows sighed. "Still it was good for you to see them."

Terrence stopped walking.

"Was it?"

"Terrence..." Mr. Willows cautioned.

"I'm serious!" Terrence objected.

"Justin, Rose, Will. Upstairs," Mrs. Willows ordered. "We need to talk with Terrence."

Justin and the twins retreated upstairs. The twins crept into Rose's room as Justin closed the bathroom door (to give the illusion that they weren't listening in) before joining them.

"Is he in trouble?" Will whispered.

"I don't know," Justin replied, leaning against the door frame.

"I don't want to visit them again for a while," Terrence said from downstairs.

"They're your parents, Mrs. Willows said gently.

"It's hard enough to be here, let alone having to go and watch them-" Terrence paused. "Watch them not remember."

"They're your family," Mr. Willows said.

"Well, maybe I don't want to see my family!" Terrence shot back.

"Terrence Jermaine Strikes," Mrs. Willows said sternly. "It's Christmas. Can we just finish the day on a high note and talk through this tomorrow?"

"No!" Rose startled at Terrence's shout. "We've been dodging this for years, let's get it out in the open!"

"Why don't you want to visit?" Mrs. Willows asked quietly.

."Because it makes me feel… confined," Terrence said. Justin knew Terrence was rubbing his palm, a nervous tic he often showed when he was anxious. "Whenever I'm here, I'm reminded of things I'd rather not think about on top of missing opportunities. Matt's dad has internships for kids our age that end up helping people get jobs when they graduate, that's what I was trying to secure over the summer."

There was a silence as Terrence's words settled over the house.

"We're your guardians Terrence," Mr. Willows finally said. "We love you and we want to see you more than twice a year."

"At the risk of my happiness?" Terrence asked. "Of my future?"

"So we're just supposed to let you leech off your friends all summer?" Mr. Willows countered.

"You'd be letting me work towards my future," Terrence sighed. "In a place where I could work on my... school stuff."

"That's fair," Mrs. Willows said softly.

Justin sank onto the floor next to Rose.

"He doesn't want to see us," Rose whispered.

"That's not true," Justin whispered back.

"Then why can't he come back?" she asked.

Justin didn't reply. He didn't have an answer.

Mr. Lains' house

The twinkling from the lights on Mr. Lains' tree snuck their way into the guest room through the cracks in the door. Even more of them danced through the door when Mr. Lains pushed it open.

277

"Terrence, can we talk?" he asked.

"Sure," Terrence said, standing and following his grandfather into the living room.

Justin sat up on the bed, wondering when the fighting would begin. To his surprise, there wasn't any. Instead, Terrence re-entered the room after twenty minutes and told Justin it was his turn.

When Justin had first seen the lights his grandfather had put up, he was surprised how much they reminded him of when they'd visited when they were little. Now they reminded him of a battle scene. The twinkling lights were reminiscent of bombs flashing all around the hero as he faced the next challenge.

"Justin," Mr. Lains motioned for him to join him on the couch. "You know that Terrence's fight with your godparents has nothing to do with you, right?"

"Yeah," Justin shrugged.

"Terrence is just experiencing a bit of FOMO: fear of missing out," Mr. Lains explained. "He's worried that his friends will forget him, or that they'll have more time to learn how to use their abilities while he's trapped at home."

Justin had had that same concern himself. However, he'd forgotten his fear the second he'd gotten home.

"It has nothing to do with you," Mr. Lains repeated. "He'll probably be visiting home more often than you think."

Chapter Twenty-Six
Another Piece of the Puzzle

"I don't think he ever plans on coming home again," Justin sighed, leaning against the wall of the passageway.

"That stinks," Eliza gave him a sympathetic look. "Wish Marian would do that."

"Was she a complete monster over break?" Justin smiled, grateful for the change of subject.

"Of course," she groaned, grabbing a buckeye (a peanut butter ball dipped in chocolate) that Ms. Wilkins had sent with Simon. "She got an array of designer beauty products then spent *hours* complaining about the colors that clashed with her complexion. She also gave me one of her old curling irons as a gift." she bit into the buckeye angrily.

"That stinks," Simon frowned.

"It's fine," Eliza shrugged. "I just need to figure out how to use it as a weapon."

Neither Justin nor Simon had a reply for that.

"My Christmas was great," Simon announced. "My brother, Brian, got me a remote control helicopter. It broke within an hour, but it was a great hour. And Claire, my sister, painted me a picture."

"What of?" Justin asked.

"Well... she claims it's a portrait of me," he blushed. "But it looks like a big blob."

"Accurate then," Justin smirked.

Eliza let out a snort.

"You can't just walk into things like that," she laughed.

The next day

"Attention students," Mr. Whitaker's voice crackled over the PA system. "All trips to Arenthia and Cafton are suspended until further notice."

Justin turned to Eliza. "There's trips to Arenthia and Cafton?"

"Yeah," she shrugged. "That's where the older students are allowed to go when they leave campus."

"Oh," he nodded. "Right."

"Arenthia has had an outbreak of a virus," Mr. Whitaker continued. "Until the outbreak is under control all outings are canceled."

"It is flu season," Simon nodded knowingly.

"Students will remain on campus unless collected by a parent or legal guardian," Mr. Whitaker finished. "And for today's quote: glück ist nicht verdient es ist gemacht."

There was a burst of static and the room filled with frenzied chatter.

"Why is everyone so upset?" Justin frowned. "This could be so much worse."

"People are dumb when it comes to privileges," Eliza declared, taking another bite of her french toast.

Room 301

"Mr. Fields?" Justin knocked on the door.

"Yes?" Mr. Fields looked up from where he sat at his desk. "Justin!" He gave him a bewildered look. "What can I do for you?"

"You'll be fine as long as you don't focus on why you're asking," Eliza said.

"Why can't you just do it?" Simon frowned.

"Because he knows I can read minds," Eliza repeated irritatedly. "I've tried, but he was too busy guarding his mind to give an honest answer. If someone who isn't one of his students asks, he won't have his guard up and he might betray something."

"Do you think the students are being poisoned?"

Mr. Fields's hands slipped, crashing into an open drawer with a loud thud.

"My goodness," Mr. Fields rubbed his throbbing hand. "Just right out with it, huh?"

"Sorry," Justin blinked, tearing his attention away from Mr. Fields's hand, which was turning red. "I was just thinking, you can read minds, so if anyone knew it would be you."

Mr. Fields allowed himself to smile at the flattery.

"Well, you're not wrong," he smiled. "However, only the medical staff and Mr. Whitaker know the truth. I haven't been near the medical staff enough to read any of their minds and Mr. Whitaker can block mind readers pretty well and I try not to hack into the mind of the man who employs me."

"Oh," Justin nodded slowly. "So you don't think there's a supervillain here?"

"No," Mr. Fields gave him a brilliant smile.

"Thank you," Justin said, bolting from the room before the thought could fully form.

"He lied," he said as soon as he arrived in the library. "He thinks there's a villain here too."

"So between him and the teachers you overheard on Halloween," Simon said. "The general consensus is that Blackglycerin *is* hiding at the school."

"Which we already knew," Eliza sighed.

"Yeah…" Simon's brow dipped into a frown. "But if they know… How haven't they found him? There are only so many people on the staff and they won't let anyone on or off of school property. How could they not have found him? Is it because they don't know about the passages?"

"It's us," Justin realized.

"What?" Eliza turned towards him.

"It's us," he repeated. "They couldn't find anything when investigating the staff so they're investigating us."

"Oh my gosh," Simon's mouth fell open. "They're investigating us."

"That's smart," Eliza nodded. "Or it would be if we didn't already know it wasn't a student."

"But they don't know that," Simon reminded her.

Justin nodded, picturing the stranger's face in his head.

"What are they going to do when they realize it's not one of us?" he wondered aloud.

"What are they going to do if they don't find him before the semester ends?" Eliza countered.

"They'll assume they've scared him off," Simon said, leaning back in his chair.

"Even if students are still being poisoned?" Justin asked.

"Well, no," Simon admitted. "Then they'd have to be forced to realize they've missed something."

"Like we have," Eliza groaned.

"On the bright side, there haven't been any incidents in the cafeteria this semester," Justin said.

Of course, they'd only been back in classes for a week, but still, the lack of incidents was something to celebrate.

"Don't jinx us," Eliza warned, pointing a threatening finger at him.

Justin rolled his eyes and wrapped his knuckles against the wooden table.

"Happy?" hasked.

"Very," Eliza laughed.

That night: dinner

"*Aaaachhoooo!*" Kyle let out a guttural sneeze.

"Gross Kyle." Annie grimaced. "You could have gotten spit on my food."

"Sorry." Kyle sniffed.

"Do you think you should go to the nurse's?" Asked Sam, one of the first-year boys Justin didn't know as well.

"Probably," Kyle said before a bout of coughing overtook him.

"I'll take you," Annie sighed, grabbing her brother by the arm and dragging him from the room.

"Poor Kyle," Bailey said, watching the twins leave. "First his parents, now him."

"What happened to his parents?" Eliza asked.

"They were sick over the break," Bailey said, picking at her food.

"How do you know that?" Simon asked.

"Our parents are friends," Bailey explained. "We would have seen them over the break if they weren't ill."

"How sick were they?" Justin asked, remembering that morning's announcement.

"I don't know," Bailey shrugged. "But it couldn't have been too bad if they let Annie and Kyle come back to Capes."

The next day

Another morning where Justin woke up too early because he rolled over on the flashlight he'd borrowed from Kyle.

"Why don't I just give it back?" he groaned inwardly.

He contemplated getting up and giving it to him.

"Oh yeah, because I'm lazy," he recalled.

"Breakfast ends in an hour," Mr. Franklins announced, poking his head into the room.

"Crap," Justin sighed. *"I'm not up as early as I thought. Might as well return Kyle's flashlight."*

He grabbed the flashlight, rolled out of bed, and made his way towards Kyle's bed. The bed was made and Kyle was nowhere to be seen.

Justin frowned and made his way out of the room.

He knocked on the door to Mr. Franklin's apartment.

"Have you seen Kyle?" he asked as Mr. Franklins opened the door.

"Kyle's sick," Mr. Franklins said, pulling on his coat. "So he's quarantining in the nurses' ward."

"Oh," Justin nodded. "That's smart. I mean, poor Kyle, but at least he's okay."

Mr. Franklins nodded.

"It's surprising how smart this school's staff can be," he smiled fondly. "Feel lucky Justin. If you were a Normie, you'd be sick too."

"Hey, no school!" Justin giggled.

"Don't celebrate too soon," Mr. Franklins shook his head, chuckling slightly. "We'd probably send homework packets home for you."

"Boo," Justin pouted, making his way back to the dorm.

"Feel lucky Justin. If you were a norm, you'd be sick too," Mr. Franklins's words echoed in his head.

Chapter Twenty-Seven
Flu Season

"Those who can see through walls are not the same as those with otherseeing," Miss Andromeda said, pacing around the circle of chairs. "I can see through walls, while Michael," Michael nodded from his seat. "Can look into his inner eye, so to speak, and see things happening in other places. Sort of like a vision in real-time."

Eliza's eyebrows raised in surprise.

"Helpful," she muttered, eyeing Michael with particular interest.

"Oh my gosh," Justin thought, half panicked, half amused. *"She's going to kidnap him for his powers and I'll go to jail as an accomplice."*

A cough brought Justin's mind back into the classroom.

"Now, for people with otherseeing," Miss Andromeda continued. "The ability gets unlocked. The first time the Ablete can use the power it's forced upon them and they have an episode. In the episode, they see flashes of a variety of different places and after the incident, they can choose to look out into their mind and see whatever they please. Most people have an episode when they're fourteen or fifteen, so we won't be diving into the power more until around then."

To Justin's surprise, Michael seemed more relieved than disheartened as he slumped down in his chair.

Lunch: a week later

"Is it just me," Simon said as they waited in line for food. "Or does the lunchroom seem emptier than usual?"

"Huh," Justin scanned the room. "That's weird."

"No it's not," Eliza said, giving them a mystified look. "More people have gotten sick, so they're staying in the nurses' ward."

"They are?" Justin and Simon frowned.

"Yeah," Eliza gave a shrug. "I heard a rumor that one of the third year girls passed out during class 'cause she had a fever."

"Really?" Justin breathed, his heart pounding.

"I mean, I don't know," Eliza admitted. "It's just a rumor."

"Well, at the least, they'll get better and school will go back to normal," Simon said optimistically. "What's the worst that could happen?"

A week later

"Attention students," Mr. Whitaker said over the PA system before first period. "Due to the number of sick students residing in the nurses' ward being over the room's capacity, we will be combining the dorm rooms. Everyone, with the exception of the eighth-years, will need to go to Valerie's office to get their new room assignment. Cloth facial coverings will be available for purchase in the cafeteria for those who would like filtered breathing and hand sanitizing will be mandatory at the beginning and end of each class."

"See what you did?" Eliza said to Simon. "You jinxed us."

"Should have knocked on wood," Justin agreed, giving Simon a fake scowl.

"There isn't any wood in the cafeteria!" Simon protested.

"Still," Eliza grumbled.

The next morning

The second-year boys who weren't sick moved into the first-years' dorm while theirs was being used as a sick ward for the first, second, and third-year boys who were ill. Mr. Gobeaux looked after the sick students on the first floor, while Mr. Franklins was responsible for all healthy students, which seemed to be stressing him out.

"Good morning!" Mr. Franklins said, walking into the room. His smile seemed to be stretched thin and for the first time, Justin noticed the worry lines that framed his eyes and mouth.

"Just a reminder that anyone who feels the tiniest bit unwell should go get checked by a doctor. You guys have an hour and a half for breakfast before the room needs to be disinfected."

Lunch

"It's weird to have people video calling into class when they're only one building away," Eliza commented.

"What's weirder is Ms. Drill trying to set up a live stream," Justin laughed.

"Hey," Simon said, sitting down across from them.

"Where'd you go?" Justin asked. "We couldn't find you after common sense class."

"I felt like I was going to throw up," Simon explained. "I was in the bathroom."

"T.M.I." Eliza said, scrunching up her nose.

"You asked," Simon shrugged.

"Shouldn't you go get that checked out?" Justin asked. "Just in case."

Simon nodded. "You're probably right."

That night

"Simon's quarantined," Justin announced as he entered the passageway behind the library.

"Does he have the thing that Arenthia has?" Eliza asked.

"No, he has a stomach virus," Justin replied, closing the entrance behind him. "They're quarantining him so we don't have two diseases going around the school."

"He doesn't have the muscle ache thing?" Eliza asked.

"Nope," Justin shook his head. "Just nausea."

"Well that's good," she paused. "Not the being sick thing, but at least he'll get better quicker. That's how most stomach viruses are."

"Yeah," Justin shrugged. "Hey!" he remembered the text he'd gotten that morning. "My grandfather said you and I can visit him. Mr. Whitaker agreed because Pop Pop doesn't leave the house often enough to get Arenthia's sickness."

"Cool," Eliza smiled. "I mean, I'll need to get Mom's permission again, but she probably won't care as long as she thinks I have friends."

"Which you don't," Justin teased. "You only have begrudged acquaintances."

"Nah," she shook her head. "We're friends."

Justin smiled. "So I think we've missed two key details about Blackglycerin."

"What?" Eliza asked, her eyes glittering with intrigue.

"Well first off," he began, sitting down on the floor. "What if Blackglycerin leaves Capes? How do we stop him then?"

"It won't matter," Eliza sat beside him. "The prophecy said it will be up to one of the first-years to stop him. So either we miss an opportunity now, or we find an opportunity later. Might as well try now. What's number two?"

"We think he has transformation, right?" Justin asked. "That he can change his appearance?"

"Right," Eliza nodded.

"Well then… Why did he choose to look the same when attending protests and riots?"

"Maybe it was just another disguise." she suggested.

"Then why *that* disguise?" Justin countered. "Why make himself stand out?"

"Maybe it was to inspire his forces," Eliza replied. "Or scare his enemies."

"Number three," Justin said, feeling a longer debate coming if he didn't change the subject.

"You said two things," Eliza protested.

"I thought of a third," he laughed. "What if we go to Amber for answers? She's the only person who might give us a legitimate answer."

The next day

Justin waited in the hall for the bell to ring. He knew it would be any second now because Eliza had worked out the exact minute he would need to leave in order to get from there to room 309 before the class ended.

Just as he began to doubt Eliza's planning skills, the bell went off.

"Amber," he called as she exited the room.

"Hey, Justin," she smiled. "What's up?"

"I need to ask you something," Justin said.

"Okay, what about?" she frowned slightly.

"I want to know some things about the teacher's search for…" he scanned the hallway. "Blackglycerin."

Her smile deepened.

"How about after dinner tonight, you and Eliza meet me in the gardens?" she offered. "I'll give y'all some answers then."

"Okay," he nodded, surprised by her quick response. "Thank you!"

"No problem!"

That night: the gardens

Amber strode into the center-most garden and nodded at Justin and Eliza.

"Hey," she said, sitting on the edge of the fountain's basin.

"Hey," Eliza nodded at her from where she sat in front of Justin.

"You two have some questions?" Amber asked.

"Yeah," Justin nodded, nerves subsiding.

"Okay," Amber nodded again. "Fire away!"

"Wait!" Eliza said, cutting off Justin's first question. "How do we know we can trust you?"

"Well, first off," Amber said, not missing a beat. "My mom delivered the prophecy. Which means she's neither likely to be affiliated with Blackglycerin nor will she be the one to stop him. And secondly, I don't think Blackglycerin would want a teenager on his team."

"Fair enough," Eliza shrugged, turning back to Justin. "Continue."

"Are the teachers searching the school for Blackglycerin?" Justin asked.

"Of course," Amber nodded seriously. "They've spent a lot of time stressing about the things they tell us not to worry about."

"Have they been investigating us?" Justin continued. "The students."

"Yes," Amber nodded.

"Crap," Eliza buried her head in her hands. "We're probably their lead suspects."

"Oh, not at all!" Amber hurried to say. "My mother's been in charge of investigating you two... And Simon."

"How'd she get away with that?" Justin asked, ignoring her correct assumption that Simon was also helping their investigation.

"Mr. Whitaker tried to split up the students randomly," she replied. "But was willing to listen to Mom's suggestions."

"So they don't think Blackglycerin is one of the teachers?" Eliza asked, removing her head from her hands.

"I guess not," Amber shrugged. "They're still keeping an eye on a couple of the teachers, but I'm not sure which ones."

"What are they going to do if they don't find him before the school year ends?" Justin asked.

"I don't know," Amber blinked, betraying her surprise for the first time. "But Mr. Whitaker seems to be under the impression he's too focused on attacking the school to even think of leaving any time soon."

Saturday

"I can't believe two more kids get sick and you're leaving for a sleepover," Luke said incredulously.

"Yeah, I'm lucky," Justin smiled to himself.

"Justin," Mr. Franklins said from the doorway. "Your grandfather's here."

Mr. Lains' house

"So kiddos, how's the investigation going?" Mr. Lains asked, handing out the food he'd ordered.

"Good," Justin said, unwrapping his sub.

"It's fine…" Eliza agreed. "Except we don't have any new information."

"That's not completely true," Justin interrupted. "Amber gave us some new information."

"But not enough to give us a new lead," Eliza argued.

"So nothing's changed?" Mr. Lains asked.

"Not really," "No," they sighed.

Later that night

Mr. Lains's snores snuck their way into the guest room.

"I know I've probably already said this," Eliza said from her bed. "But your grandfather's really cool."

"He is," Justin agreed.

"You're really lucky, Justin," she said quietly, moving to sit in a fetal position. "My grandparents are just worse versions of my parents. Status obsessed, with no status of their own. They dote over their eldest, while their other children fight for attention."

"I'm sorry," Justin said.

"Thanks," she looked down at the bed. "I just wish they'd pay more attention. Especially now that Kara and April are home alone with them."

"They'll be okay without you, E," Justin said, testing out the nickname. "They still have you, even if you're away."

She didn't respond to the reassurance or the nickname.

"Besides," he continued. "Your parents still love you, even if it doesn't feel that way. And even if they didn't, other people do. I mean, you have a ton of friends at school and you haven't even been there a year yet, the teachers adore you, and you have me and Simon."

Eliza looked up and gave him a watery smile.

"Thanks, Justin."

"Anytime," he promised.

Chapter Twenty-Eight
The Inflictor

One month later

Nothing new had been discovered, even after Simon had gotten better. To make things worse, whatever virus had overtaken a majority of the school continued to spread. Some students were only sick for a couple of days, others were sick for a month. Almost everyone, including the staff, had gotten it, including Eliza, who was sick for a week, and Kyle, who caught it three times.

Capes had drastically changed since Justin had first arrived. More and more people started wearing masks in class, handwashing had become mandatory before and after every class and meal, and there were fewer mixed-ages in groups of people hanging out. The biggest change was in the cafeteria.

"Yes!" Simon cheered. "Pizza again!"

One of the fourth-years behind them groaned.

"I wish we were having chicken nuggets," Eliza said longingly.

"Could be worse," Justin shrugged, grabbing a plate. "Could be poisoned."

"Well okay, yeah," Eliza rolled her eyes. "When you put it *that* way I have to feel grateful for having pizza the third time this week."

"Also we had chicken nuggets for lunch yesterday," Simon smirked.

"Yeah," Eliza sighed dreamily.

Justin laughed.

"I hope we get tacos again," Luke said from in front of them.

"I wish we'd get Sandwich Wednesday back," Bailey said glumly. "Or spaghetti night."

"If Blackglycerin isn't caught, we might never have spaghetti night again," Justin realized.

"If he isn't caught," a voice whispered back. *"The school might close."*

That night

"Light on… There it goes," Justin beamed as the bathroom light turned on. *"And off."*

The bathroom light flickered then the room went dark.

"And back on," he muttered.

302

Nothing happened. Justin was stuck in darkness.

"Okay, don't panic," he whispered to himself, reaching forward.

He felt his way across the wall and to the counter. He moved his hands to the cabinets and made his way towards the door, hands creeping across the fake cabinets as he inched his way closer to the light shining under the door.

"Well, it's a good thing I'm not afraid of the dark," he thought. *"Otherwise this would totally freak me ou-"*

His train of thought was lost as his fingers met a familiar abrasive surface.

Justin blinked in surprise. The lights flickered on.

"The dorm entrance is in the bathroom?" he frowned, vaguely surprised by the occurrence. He'd passed out before they'd opened the dorm entrances and, despite the fact Eliza used the tunnels frequently, he'd never thought to ask where the entrance was.

"It's not curfew yet," he thought. *"But I probably shouldn't explore alone."*

He ran a hand over the panel.

"On the other hand… I have no reason not to…"

He crouched down and pushed against the panel, muscles straining as the panel popped open into the cabinet.

The fake front of the cabinet creaked open, revealing the dark entrance to the passages.

Justin reached up, grabbed his electric toothbrush off the counter, and glanced up at the overhead lights.

He closed his eyes, unsure how long it would take for this to work if it did at all. After a minute, he couldn't wait anymore and opened his eyes.

The little light on his toothbrush was glowing with a brilliantly bright glow.

"Cool," he smiled, shining the light into the cubbyhole.

The inside of the cabinet was small and dirty and there were footholds directly across from the opening.

Justin held the toothbrush in his mouth and crawled into the cupboard, the blue glow from his toothbrush the only source of light as the entrance closed behind him.

Justin scooted forward to where the footholds were. He took the toothbrush from his mouth and scanned the area. There was a forked tunnel to his left and when he looked up, he saw a path that made its way to the other dorms.

Justin turned and looked down the forked tunnel. The tunnel to the main building was lit, but the one leading to the fountain wasn't.

Justin frowned. He wasn't sure how the light in the passages worked, but Simon had assumed that they were activated when someone pulled one of the levers, that's why the tunnel from the rec building to here wasn't lit, it didn't have a lever. But if that was the case, why was only one of the halls lit?

Justin felt like he had a pit in his stomach as he realized the answer.

"Someone's in the passages."

He slid his toothbrush into his pocket, took a deep breath, and formed a shield over himself as he headed down the hallway.

"Be quiet, don't be seen, don't get caught." He thought to himself.

At first, nothing seemed off. There weren't any obvious signs of someone using the passage, no sounds other than his own footsteps, and he didn't see anything in front of him. Nothing seemed to be any different than the last time he'd been in this passage.

Then he heard a faint whisper and stopped dead in his tracks. He pressed himself against the wall and listened carefully.

"No," the whisper said. "Of course I haven't. It isn't time yet. I'm waiting an hour and then planting the virus in Mr. Whitaker's office, just as planned. I'm not stupid."

Justin held his breath and snuck along the length of the wall.

"I'll be in and out," the lurker continued. "It's not like it's my first time doing this. I've been doing this all year. Have some faith in me."

Justin peeked around the corner, stopping long enough to see who was talking before jumping back into his hiding place.

"It's the guy I saw in the hallway!" he realized, heart rate quickening.

"Breathe," he told himself. *"Remember the important details. An hour. Mr. Whitaker's office. The virus... I should go!"* he realized. *"We have a time and place to catch him!"*

He quietly, but quickly, made his way back to the bathroom.

He could feel the stress trying to get to him as he climbed out of the cabinet, but he was too focused to care.

He began to race out of the room but stopped, put his toothbrush back on the counter before sprinting out of the room.

"Simon!" he said, as soon as he spotted him in the rec room. "Do you remember where Eliza said she'd be?"

"The movie room, why?" Simon blinked.

"I'll tell you when we find her," Justin said, running out of the room, Simon hot on his heels.

Justin was out of breath before he even entered the back building. The feeling only multiplied by a hundred after he ran up three flights of stairs.

With his lungs feeling like they'd been through a wood chipper, he peeked into the movie room and waved to get Eliza's attention.

"What?" she asked as she closed the door behind her.

"I found him," Justin panted. "He's in the passages. He's planning on releasing the virus in Mr. Whitaker's office in an hour."

"What?" Simon gasped, eyes wide and eyebrows raised.

"Slow down," Eliza ordered. "Are you sure it's him?"

"Not really," Justin said, forcing himself to breathe. "He's talking to someone… I think. He was talking about planting the virus in Mr. Whitaker's office."

"So we know a time and place where he'll be!" Simon exclaimed.

"Yeah," Justin nodded. "So do we tell an adult?"

"And risk people knowing about the passages?" Eliza asked.

"She doesn't have to know," Simon said, leading their way downstairs. "You can tell her you had a vision of the culprit coming out of the supply closet."

"She?" Eliza frowned.

"Mrs. Strong," the boys said, running across the lawn to the main building.

Chapter Twenty-Nine
Capturing the Culprit

Mrs. Strong blinked in surprise.

"And you know this because…" she paused.

"Eliza had a vision," Justin said stupidly.

"About an hour ago," Eliza added.

Mrs. Strong turned to Simon, who was brewing in guilty silence. Mrs. Strong raised an eyebrow at him but didn't ask him to confirm his friends' half-lies.

"Well," she said, rising to her feet as she turned her gaze back to Justin and Eliza. "We better get going if we're going to catch him in time."

She made her way out of the room, cardigan flowing behind her as she mounted the stairs, skipping two steps at a time.

Mr. Whitaker's office

"So they believe he'll be here in twenty-five minutes?" Mr. Whitaker asked.

"We *know* he will be," Eliza glared at him.

Mr. Whitaker blinked at her, not at all intimidated by her outburst. Probably because he had met hundreds of angry hormonal teenagers just like her.

"So what's your plan?" he asked, turning back to Mrs. Strong.

"You wait here," she started. "I wait in Valerie's office... I believe Mr. Crain is still here?"

"He is as far as I know," Mr. Whitaker nodded.

"He'll wait in Andromeda's office and try and flush him into our corridor," she motioned with her hands. "We make sure he doesn't evade capture."

"What about us?" Justin asked.

Mr. Whitaker startled at them, having obviously forgotten that he and Simon were there in the wake of Eliza's outburst.

Mrs. Strong gave them a knowing smile.

"The nurse's wing," she said pleasantly. "In case he runs that way."

"Elizabeth," Mr. Whitaker frowned. "Should we really let-"

"Yes, Erik," she gave him an identical smile to the one she'd just given Justin and Simon. "These three can be trusted, I've foreseen it."

"Why is she lying?" Justin thought, trying not to show his confusion.

"Maybe she's not."

"Very well," Mr. Whitaker nodded. "Go get Mr. Crain and tell him your plan, I'll escort these three to a good…" he glanced at them. "Stakeout spot."

Eliza gave a breathy snort.

"Wonderful," Mrs. Strong spun around and fled from the room.

Nurses' ward

"Are we really going to wait here?" Eliza whispered from behind the nurse's desk.

"No," Simon rolled his eyes from his spot behind the door. "But we're waiting until we're sure they won't come check on us first."

"Is that what we're doing?" Justin frowned at the coatrack he was behind.

Simon giggled.

"Whatever," Eliza sighed, standing up and making her way to the door. She poked her head out of the door.

"No sign of anyone," she whispered.

"Well, maybe I got the time wrong," Justin shrugged. "I could be off by a couple minutes."

Eliza shushed him.

"Someone's coming," she mouthed.

Footsteps sounded in the hall as the intruder made their way towards the office. Justin could hear his heartbeat quickening as the footsteps made their way up the stairs and into the hall.

A click sounded in the hallway and the footsteps stopped.

Simon inclined his head to the door. Eliza gave him a nod and peeked out the door.

"He's stopped," she mouthed.

"Why?" Justin frowned.

"I don't know," Eliza peeked out the door again.

"Guys," Simon waved to get their attention. *"What if he somehow avoids the teachers?"*

A door slammed from down the hall; Mr. Crain's attempt to flood the intruder into the office.

The footsteps sounded again, this time becoming louder, the pace quickened in the prowler's frightened state.

Justin turned to his friends.

"He's coming this way," he looked at Eliza. *"Block the exit. Simon, watch my back."*

Eliza gave a sharp nod, the blue streak in her hair rippling red. Justin nodded back, took a deep breath, and stepped into the hall.

"What the-" the intruder, the same one that Justin had seen remembered in his flashback, stared at him in shock.

Justin used the stranger's surprise to his advantage. He enclosed his opposer in a force field as Eliza came out of the nurse's ward, a white bed sheet flapping behind her.

Justin felt a bruising sensation in his left arm as the trespasser slammed his body against the shield. The shield turned a paler shade of blue but held firm against the attack.

"Hurry, please," Justin said as Eliza unfolded the sheet.

Eliza threw the sheet past the encaptured culprit, using her telekinesis to make it fly down the hall.

The imposter broke free from the shield and ran down the hall as Justin collapsed to the floor.

"I'm okay," Justin panted as Simon ran to his side. "Cover Eliza."

Eliza spread her hands and the sheet expanded at the end of the hall, successfully blocking the intruder's path.

The fiend glared at them over his shoulder before he tried to punch the sheet. The sheet, however, stood firm. He mumbled something to himself and held his hand up. He set his hand ablaze and pressed his palm to the sheet.

"Guys!" Eliza's voice wavered as the sheet set on fire.

"Mrs. Strong!" Justin called to the teacher.

"No no no..." Simon muttered, running towards the intruder as the hole in the fabric became big enough for him to escape through.

Simon stopped halfway down the hall and held his arms out and flipped his palms down.

A green portal opened underneath the villain's feet, he fell into the void. Simon stared in shock at the feat he'd accomplished, then turned his hands palm up. Another portal opened above the first one. The intruder fell out of the top portal right into the one on the floor, catching himself in a never-ending loop.

Mrs. Strong emerged from the office and stared at the scene before her; Simon's hands stretched out, Justin on the floor, the intruder falling through the portals, the flaming sheet; and gave an airy laugh.

"Marvelous!" she gave them a nod, eyes still laughing as the intruder tried to use a column of flames to try and stop his fall.

"Mr. Whitaker!" she called into the room behind her. "Our helpers have caught our culprit!"

She walked over to where Justin lay on the floor and helped him stand.

"You used a force field?" she asked.

"Yeah," he nodded, still feeling a tad dizzy as he stood.

Mr. Whitaker entered the hall and gave the room an opened mouth stare. Eliza was opening and closing one of her hands making the sheet pat the flames out.

Mr. Whitaker blinked at her, then went to fetch Mr. Crain.

"I'll take it from here, dear," Mrs. Strong said to Simon, touching him gently on the shoulder. "Just wait until he disappears through the floor, vanish the portal and I'll open a new one. Then we do the same thing with the top one, okay?"

Simon nodded, his eyes glued to the portals.

The suspect disappeared into the void. Simon shook his left hand and the bottom portal vanished. Mrs. Strong waved a hand and a glowing purple portal took the vacant spot.

"Are you sure you're okay?" Eliza whispered as Simon got rid of the top portal.

"Not really," Justin admitted. "You?"

"I think I'm okay," she shrugged.

Mr. Whitaker reentered the hall followed by a slow-moving Mr. Crain.

"Have you identified him?" he asked, eyeing the trespasser as he continued to fall.

"I was waiting for the two of you," Mrs. Strong gave him a smile. "Eliza and Justin."

She turned to face them.

"Would you two bring a mattress and some bandages?"

"Yes ma'am," they nodded, dashing into the nurse's ward.

Justin grabbed a roll of cloth bandages from the nurse's desk and turned to Eliza.

"This one," she declared.

Justin shoved the bandages into his back pocket and stood at the foot of the bed.

"I get the end, you get the front?" he suggested.

"Sure," she held out a hand and lifted the head of the mattress using telekinesis.

Justin placed a hand under his end of the bed and did the same.

"Wonderful!" Mrs. Strong smiled as they re-entered the hallway, her left hand still held aloft to maintain the portals. "I'm going to get rid of the bottom portal and you're going to slide the mattress under the top portal."

They dropped the mattress next to the portal on the floor.

"Ready?" she asked.

"Ready," the trio nodded.

They watched as the intruder fell through the floor. Mrs. Strong's bracelets jingled as she vanished the portal with a wave of her hand.

The mattress slid a little past its mark, but Simon straightened it as the offender fell from the ceiling one last time.

"Ow!" the culprit exclaimed, grabbing his ribs.

"Where are the bandages?" Mr. Whitaker asked as Mr. Crain grabbed the man by the arms.

"Here," Justin tossed them to him.

"I know you don't I?" Mr. Whitaker asked as he began to tie up the villain's hands.

"I don't have to answer without a lawyer," the man said gruffly.

"We're not cops, son," Mr. Crain rolled his eyes. "And the Ablete Miranda Laws allow us to have our own investigation before we hand you over to the authorities."

"Who are you?" Mr. Whitaker asked.

"Bobby," Mrs. Strong nodded at the boy. "Bobby Flaunt."

"You were expelled!" Mr. Whitaker's eyes widened as he remembered.

"Erik," Mr. Crain interrupted. "We should do this somewhere private."

Mr. Whitaker looked at Justin, Eliza, and Simon and nodded.

"Right," he nodded. "Get up," he ordered Bobby, hoisting him to a kneeling position.

"Wait, we want to know what's going on!" Eliza interjected.

"You'll find out one way or another," Mrs. Strong gave them a wink. "The walls have ears."

She followed the other teachers into the office and closed the door.

"The wall!" Simon realized. He ran to the end of the hall and pressed an ear to the wall. "We can hear the interrogation!" he whispered loudly, motioning them over.

Justin and Eliza raced to join him at the wall, falling silent as they listened in to another conversation they weren't supposed to hear.

Chapter Thirty
The Interrogation

"Lester, hold him in place," Mr. Whitaker ordered. "I'm going to tie him to the chair. Elizabeth, guard the door."

Justin had assumed Mr. Whitaker wasn't very authoritative because of how much he fumbled during morning announcements. However, he seemed to know exactly what to say to get his team to listen to him.

"I had wondered what happened to you after you attempted to blow up the dining hall," Mrs. Strong said to Bobby.

"I thought the government was supposed to keep an eye on scoundrels like you," Mr. Crain growled.

"I'm not a scoundrel," Bobby grunted. "I'm a biochemist."

"Really?" Mr. Whitaker asked. "Because I thought that attacking a school made you a domestic terrorist."

Bobby didn't respond.

"A biochemist," Mrs. Strong said wonderingly. "Do you work on vaccines? That would allow you access to the ingredients you'd need to make a virus."

Bobby gave a low laugh. "It's amazing how much people trust you when they think you're a genius."

"So it *was* you who had been poisoning our students," Mr. Whitaker said. "And you who spread the virus at the school?"

"Originally I had tried to spread it to Arenthia," Bobby admitted. "That way you couldn't source it back to me."

"Smart," Mrs. Strong said, complimenting his brain more than his villainy.

"Would have worked too if it wasn't for your little quarantine rule," Bobby sighed, remorsefully.

"Why though?" Mr. Whitaker asked. "Why were you attacking our students?"

"I was recruited to," Bobby said, no doubt smirking at their slowness.

"By who?" Mr. Crain asked.

"You already know who," Bobby said.

"Blackglycerin," Mrs. Strong stated knowingly.

"Is he here?" Mr. Whitaker asked sharply.

"Oh, most indefinitely," Bobby laughed.

"Who is he?" Mr. Crain asked.

"I dunno," Bobby said slowly.

"How could you not know?" Mr. Whitaker asked suspiciously.

"He has his disguises," Bobby said evasively. "Doesn't trust anyone on his team to see who he's undercover as."

"What's he doing here?" Mrs. Strong asked.

"He has a grand purpose," Bobby monologued. "First he reforms this school, then America, then the world. The world as we know it will be destroyed and this building will stand as a monument to his achievement."

"It would take a lot to reform Capes, let alone the world," Mr. Whitaker laughed darkly.

"All it takes is one generation," Bobby countered. "One generation that's willing to open their eyes."

Silence settled in the office as the teachers tried to think of what else they needed to know.

"How have you evaded us for so long?" Mrs. Strong asked.

"I got to know this school very well in my five years as a student," he answered. "I know all sorts of cubbyholes you've never discovered. I can get from here to the main gate and never enter the main hallway."

"The passages," Justin whispered. Eliza nodded her agreement.

"What will Blackglycerin do next?" Mr. Whitaker asked.

"No clue," Bobby said remorsefully. "He doesn't tell his people the whole plan, just what their role is, it's how he keeps his plan from falling apart."

"We should go," Justin said as the teachers ignored his monologue and began to call the Arenthian police.

"Right," Simon and Eliza agreed.

The left fountain in front of Capes

"What if Bobby *is* Blackglycerin?" Simon worried.

"He would have put up more of a fight," Justin pointed out.

"And Blackglycerin wouldn't have given up everything he knew," Eliza added.

"Unless that was Blackglycerin and he does know more!" Simon gave an exasperated sigh.

Police lights flashed from the Capes gates.

"What if Blackglycerin breaks Bobby out of jail?" Justin asked.

"He probably won't," Eliza replied, tugging on a strand of her hair as she watched the teachers escorted Bobby to the police. "I doubt Blackglycerin needs him for whatever part of his scheme is next."

Justin watched as the police put cuffs on Bobby, who smirked the whole time.

"I wonder if *he* knows that," Justin thought out loud as the police put Bobby in the back of one of their cars.

Mrs. Strong made her way towards them.

"Wonderful job tonight, children," she praised. "That was the most impressive display of abilities I've ever seen from any of the first-years. However," she sighed, glancing over her shoulder to where Mr. Whitaker and Mr. Crain stood talking to the cops. "If we ever have another situation like this, I think it'd be best if you three try and stay out of harm's way."

Justin nodded disheartenedly. He'd known this was coming, but it didn't make it any harder to agree to.

"Don't worry," Mrs. Strong gave them a smile. "You'll have plenty of time for hero work when you're older."

Eliza nodded, still trying to get Mrs. Strong to take back her subtle reprimand as she stared at the teacher with puppy dog eyes. If Mrs. Strong noticed the look, she didn't acknowledge it. Instead, she gave them another smile before heading back to the main building.

The trio watched in silence as the flickering halo of red and blue faded into the distance. Mr. Whitaker gave them a nod as he and Mr. Crain made their way back to their offices.

"What now?" Simon asked.

"We find Blackglycerin," Eliza squared her shoulders.

"How?" Simon frowned.

"We find the piece of the puzzle that we're missing," Justin shrugged.

"And that's…"

"Who is he pretending to be," Eliza answered.

"Once we know how he's hiding we can find where he's hiding and who he's hiding as," Justin checked his phone. "We should get to the dorms, it's almost curfew."

Eliza nodded, scanning the school grounds.

"Meet me in the passage behind room 108 in an hour," she said.

"Why?" Simon frowned.

"We deserve to celebrate," she smirked.

Chapter Thirty-One
Heading Home

The sun seemed as if it would never shine again. Terror and anxiety settled amidst the students once more. Exam week was not to be trifled with.

"Grades will be sent home by mid-June," Mr. Quakes reminded his earth science class as he passed out their final exam. "So don't stress out about your grade until then. Start when you're ready."

Justin stared at the papers in front of him as if they were written in another language. He snuck a glance at his friends. Eliza was frowning at her paper but had already circled three answers and Simon was flying through his pages. Justin sighed and began to work through the questions.

The next day: distinct abilities

"Madeline and I just wanted to tell you how proud we are," Mrs. Strong said as everyone settled into the classroom. "First-year distinct abilities doesn't have as much hands-on experience as the later years, yet your class has been able to activate and control your abilities in some way."

She winked at Eliza and Justin.

"Yes," Miss Andromeda nodded. "And we are so excited to see what you can achieve next year."

"Now, for the last class of the year," Mrs. Strong continued. "We're going to take a look at the last of Eliza's powers; her ability to change her appearance."

Eliza nodded, running a hand through her hair, prompting her blue streak to turn green.

"Like that," Mrs. Strong gestured towards Eliza's highlight as it reverted to its normal color.

"However, those with transformation have different tiers of how powerful they are," Miss Andromeda explained. "Someone Eliza's age could change their hair or eye color, someone a couple years older could choose to steal someone else's entire look. Some adults could change not only *their* identity but someone else's as well."

Justin audibly gasped, falling into a trance as the realization hit him. In fact, he was so deep in his trance that he at first didn't hear Mrs. Strong calling his name at the end of class.

"Justin?" she repeated.

"Yes!" he blinked his trance away.

"I gathered some information about your mother," she said, opening a folder to show him. "Sorry it took so long."

"That's okay," Justin stared at the forms and pictures sitting inside the folder.

"It's mostly clipping from school newspapers," Mrs. Strong told him. "Along with old report cards and a couple entries from the diary I used to keep."

"Wow!" Justin accepted the folder and blinked up at her. "Thank you, Mrs. Strong."

"Anytime," she gave him a pat on the back.

Justin hugged the folder to his chest and ran to his next class.

"Where were you?" Bailey whispered as he slid into his seat.

"I had to talk to Mrs. Strong," he replied.

Miss Drills hushed them. Bailey gave Justin an impish smile. Justin suppressed a giggle, completely forgetting about the revelation he'd had.

Departure day

The main building and front lawn were both jam-packed with students waiting to be taken back home. Justin, Eliza, and Simon had escaped to the one vacant spot on campus, the gardens.

"I forgot!" Justin exclaimed as Eliza tried to find her headphones in her suitcase.

"Forgot what?" Simon asked, jumping at his friend's outburst.

"Eliza, remember yesterday's distinct abilities class?" Justin ignored Simon's question.

"Yeah?" she frowned.

"What if someone is changing Blackglycerin's appearance for him?" he asked.

Eliza's eyes widened.

"Oh my gosh," she gasped. "That's why he's at Capes. His cohort is here and he needs to keep an eye on them."

Simon opened his mouth to say something but was cut off as someone entered the garden.

"Great, there you are," Marian rolled her eyes at her sister. "Mom's here, we're leaving."

Eliza sighed. "I'll be right there."

Marian had already spun on her heel and was walking away.

Eliza turned back to them, a sad look plastered on her face.

"I've got to go," she said lamely.

They stared at her in silence.

"Well…" Simon coughed. "We'll see you next year."

"Right," Eliza nodded.

"I'll email you as soon as I get home," Justin promised.

"You better," Eliza waved her finger at him threateningly. "Otherwise I'll hunt you down in Tennessee and personally slap you."

Justin laughed. "Okay."

"We won't forget about you," Simon pointed out. "Besides, we'll never find Blackglycerin without you."

"True," Eliza shouldered her bag. "I should go. I'll see you next year."

"See you next year," Justin and Simon chorused as she turned to leave.

Half an hour later

Simon's mom had picked him up ten minutes ago and Justin, now alone, decided to go to the main building to see if anyone he knew was still there.

"Justin!" Peyton called to him as he entered the building.

Justin jolted for a split second, then walked over to where Peyton stood by the stairwell with Terrence and Matt.

"Heading back to the Willows'?" Terrence asked.

"Yeah," Justin nodded. "Heading to Matt's?"

"Yup!" Terrence feigned indifference, but the sparkle in his eyes gave away his excitement. "But hey! You should join us at camp before next semester starts."

"Yeah!" Matt gave Justin an over-enthusiastic nod. "You'll also love next year at Capes. It's Ablete game season."

"What's Ablete game season?" Justin frowned.

Terrence and Matt shared an elfish grin.

"You'll see," Peyton promised.

"I'll send Ma the camp information," Terrence continued, pulling out his phone. "I think you'd really like it there."

"Okay..." Justin frowned at Matt, who was watching him with a wild grin.

"Justin?" someone called from behind him.

Justin turned. Miss Andromeda was standing in the doorway looking for him.

"Here!" he waved at her.

"Your grandfather is here."

120 Two Bridges Street

Justin sat up from where he'd been crouching in his closet and patted the spot where his school books were hidden.

Returning home reminded him how dull normal life was compared to life at Capes. Even without the craziness of Blackglycerin, Capes was always alive. Whereas Capes was constantly noisy, the Willows's house was quiet other than the few outbursts.

Someone knocked on the door, sending Justin tumbling backward in surprise.

"Justin?" Rose called from the hall.

"Just a second!" he shouted, scrambling to get up.

"Mom wants to know if you wanna go see a movie with us," Rose said as Justin slammed his closet door shut.

Justin opened the door to find Rose frowning.

"What were you doing?" she asked.

"Reading," he shrugged.

"Mom says we're leaving in ten minutes," Rose said, squinting at him from behind her glasses. "You

332

can't come if you're going to continue slamming books shut so loudly."

Justin smiled. "Noted."

His phone buzzed from where it sat on his desk. He went to check it as Rose retreated back downstairs.

1 new email: E.T.ishere@mailonline.site

did u hear the news about the ablete games? -eliza

"Justin!" Mrs. Willows called from downstairs. "If you're coming with us, you need to be getting ready."

"Coming, Ma!" Justin replied.

He glanced back at Eliza's email. Maybe regular life felt kind of boring, but Justin had a hunch that the feeling wouldn't last long.

About The Author

A.C "Abby" Ham is an eighteen-year-old, Athens based artist who discovered her love for writing short stories and poetry during her senior year of high school. While writing is one of her passions, she spends a majority of her time drawing and painting, all while singing whatever song happens to be stuck in her head.

A.C on social media:

Instagram: officialjustinstrikes (&) cartripcomics

Tumblr: therealabbyham

Special Thanks

Paula Semple, for being my teacher, answering all of my questions, and helping make this process as smooth as possible.

Samantha J. Cowart, you're one of my favorite fellow writers, thank you for helping me edit this mess and for hyping up my work. You love Eliza as much as I do and that alone means the world.

My parents, Dave and Jess, for letting me be wrapped up in this world I created while preparing me for the real world.

To my favorite authors, for creating worlds I can't wait to go back to and inspiring me to do the same thing for someone else.

Huge shout out to Caden, for making this better (or at least grammatically better) version of the book. Seriously, I appreciated it a lot and I'm grateful for all the questions and suggestions :)

And to God, for helping me make it to this point.